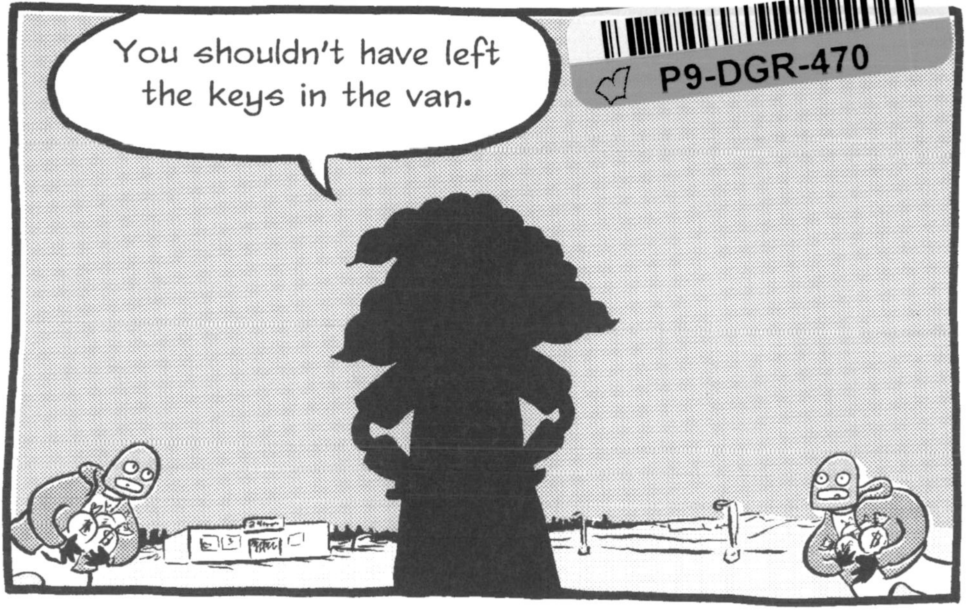
You shouldn't have left the keys in the van.

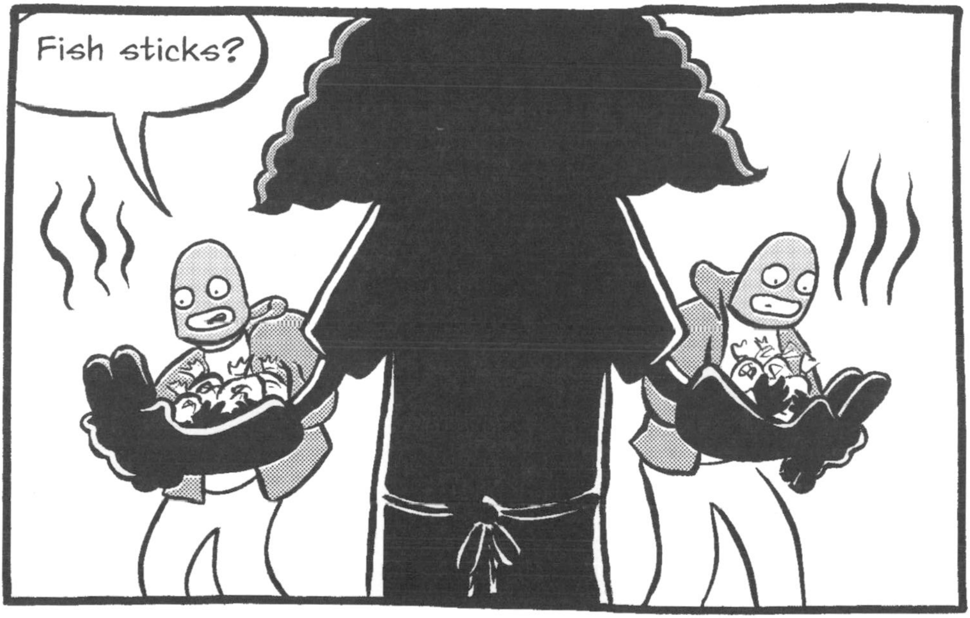
Fish sticks?

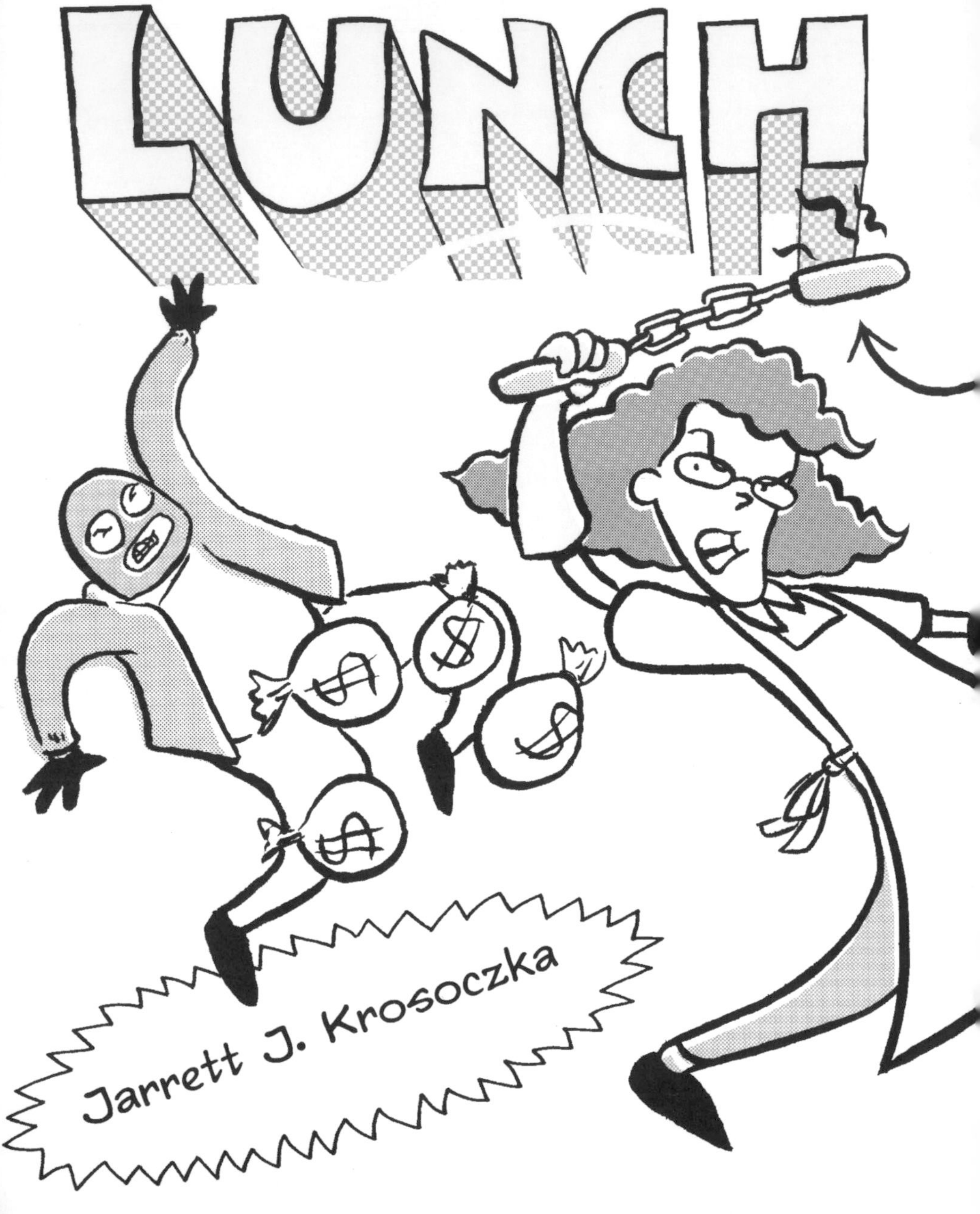
LUNCH
Jarrett J. Krosoczka

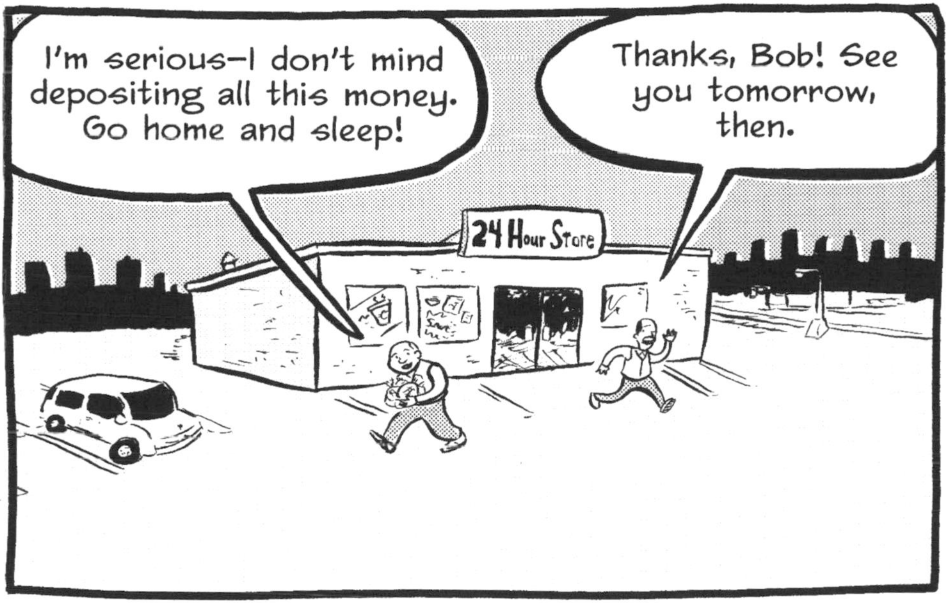
I'm serious—I don't mind depositing all this money. Go home and sleep!
Thanks, Bob! See you tomorrow, then.
24 Hour Store

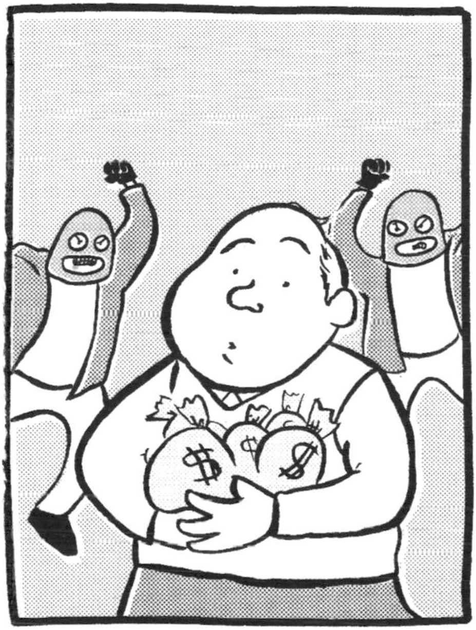

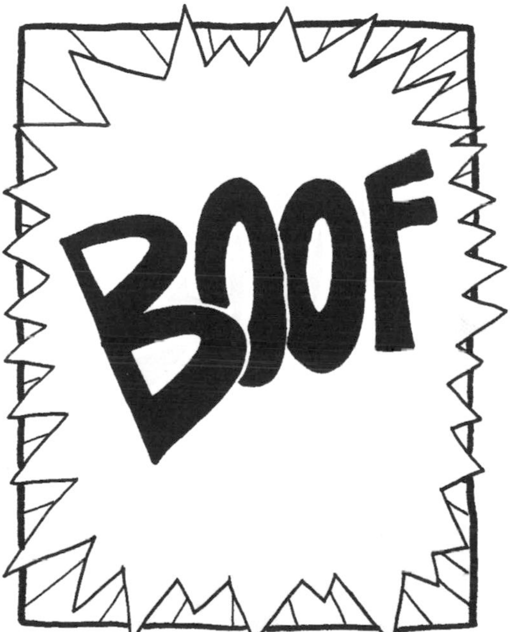
BOOF

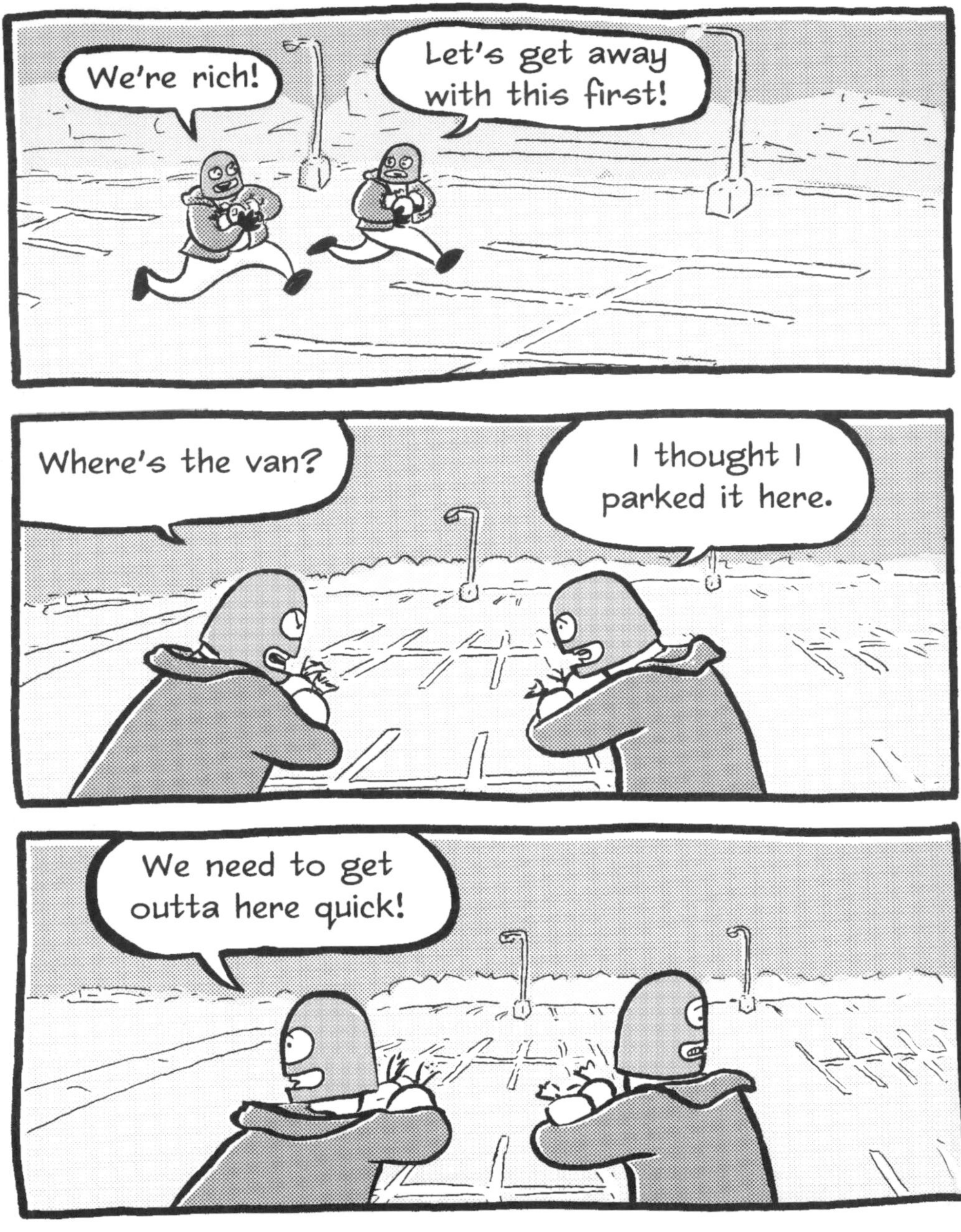
We're rich!
Let's get away with this first!
Where's the van?
I thought I parked it here.
We need to get outta here quick!

LADY and the Summer Camp Shakedown

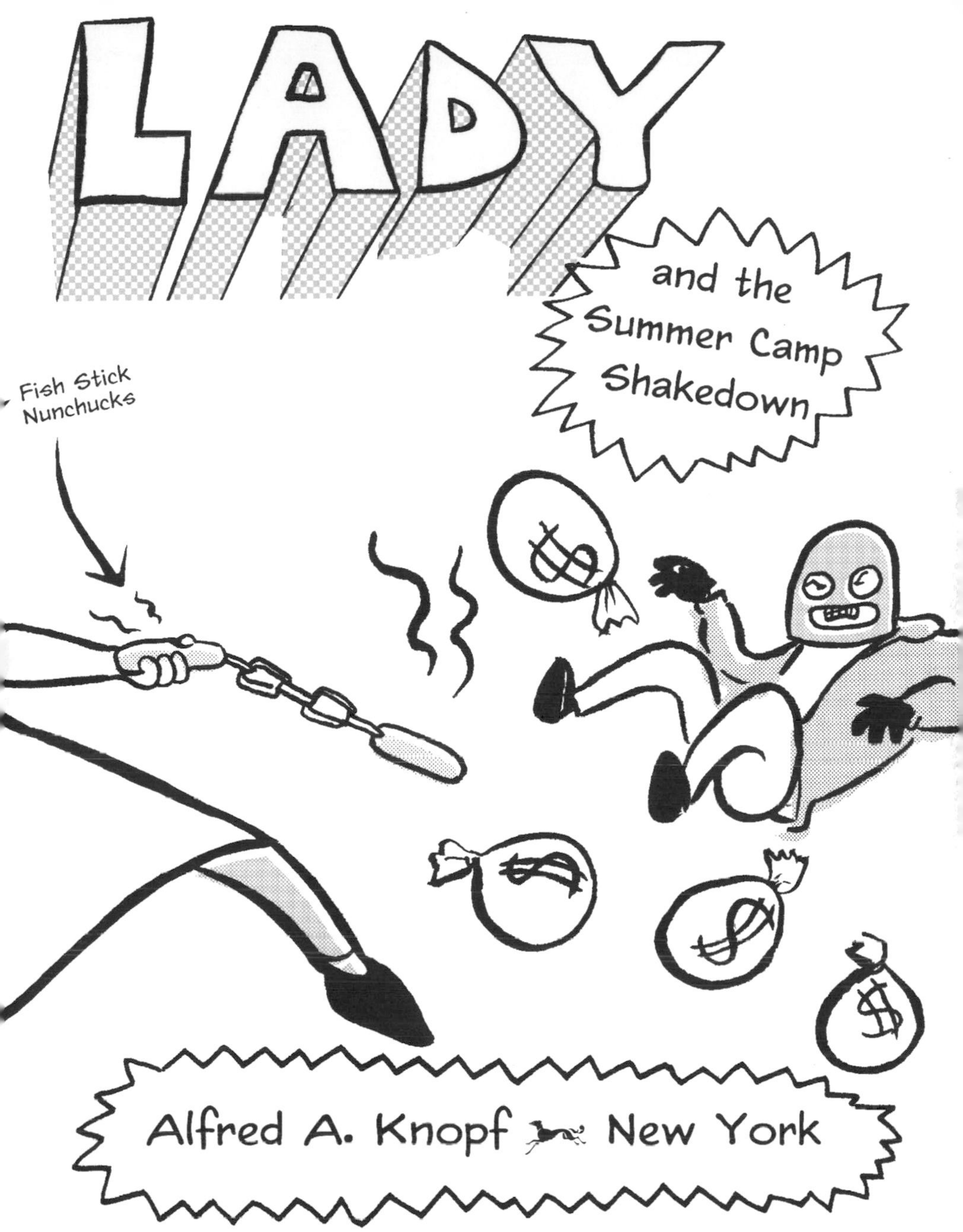
Fish Stick Nunchucks

Alfred A. Knopf New York

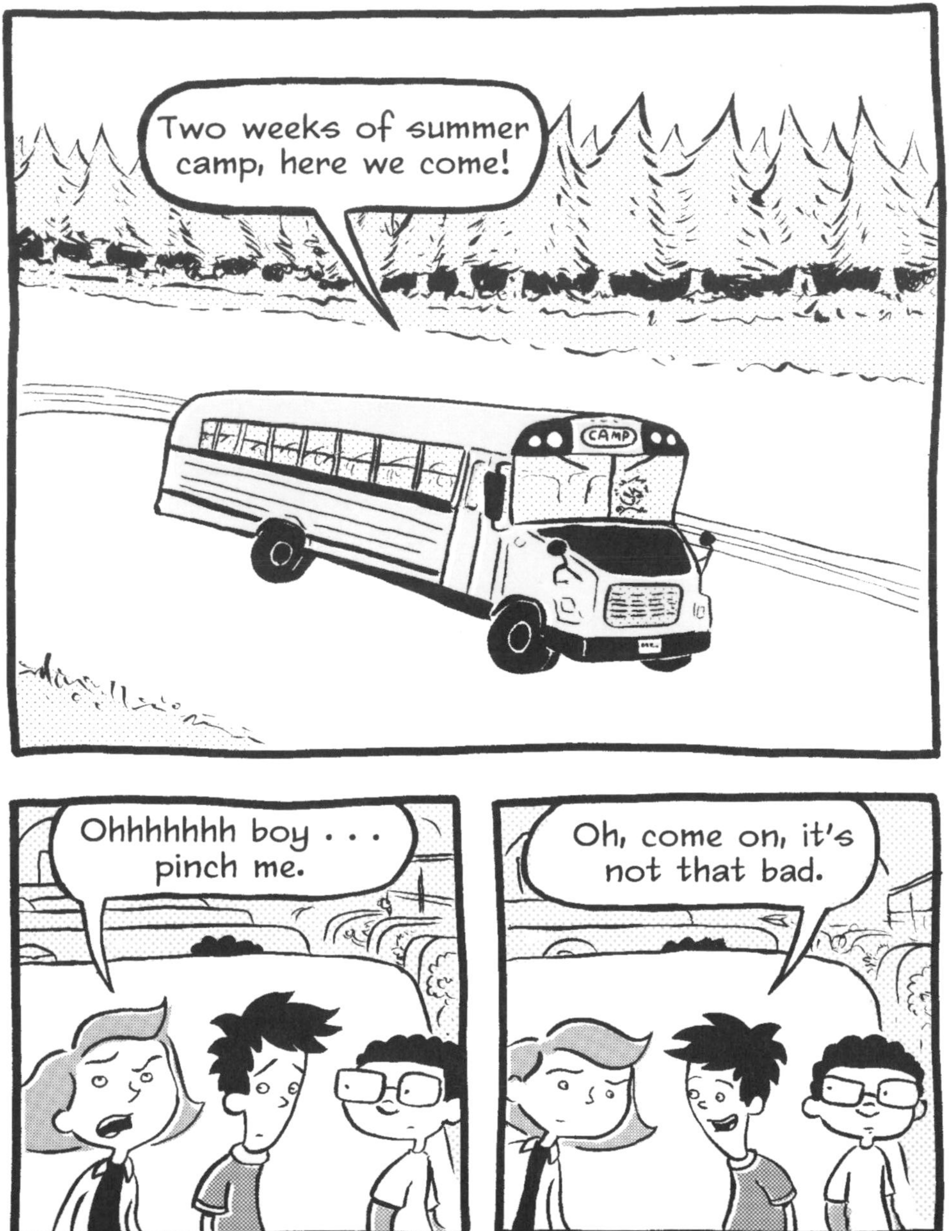
Two weeks of summer camp, here we come!
CAMP
Ohhhhhhh boy . . . pinch me.
Oh, come on, it's not that bad.

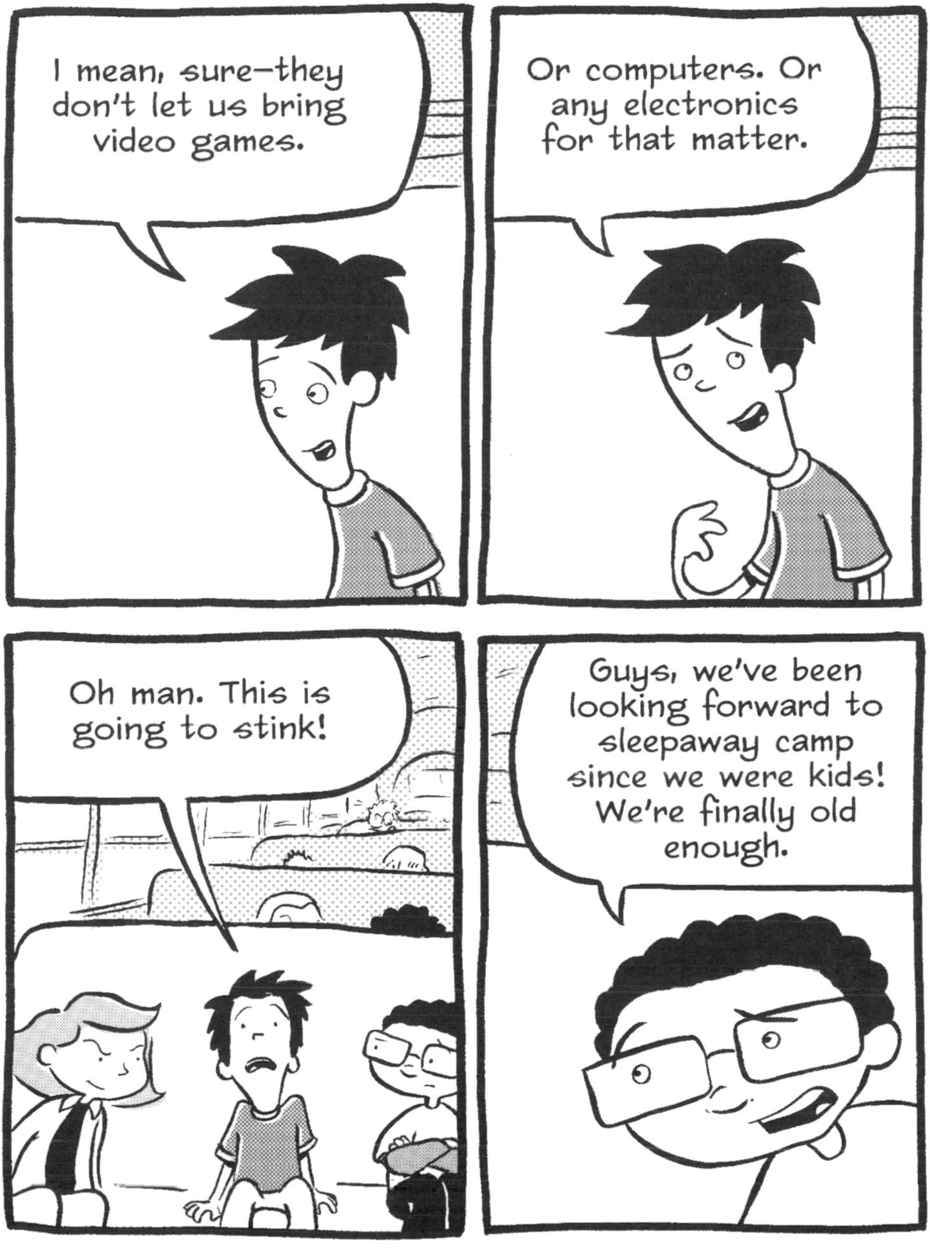
I mean, sure—they don't let us bring video games.
Or computers. Or any electronics for that matter.
Oh man. This is going to stink!
Guys, we've been looking forward to sleepaway camp since we were kids! We're finally old enough.

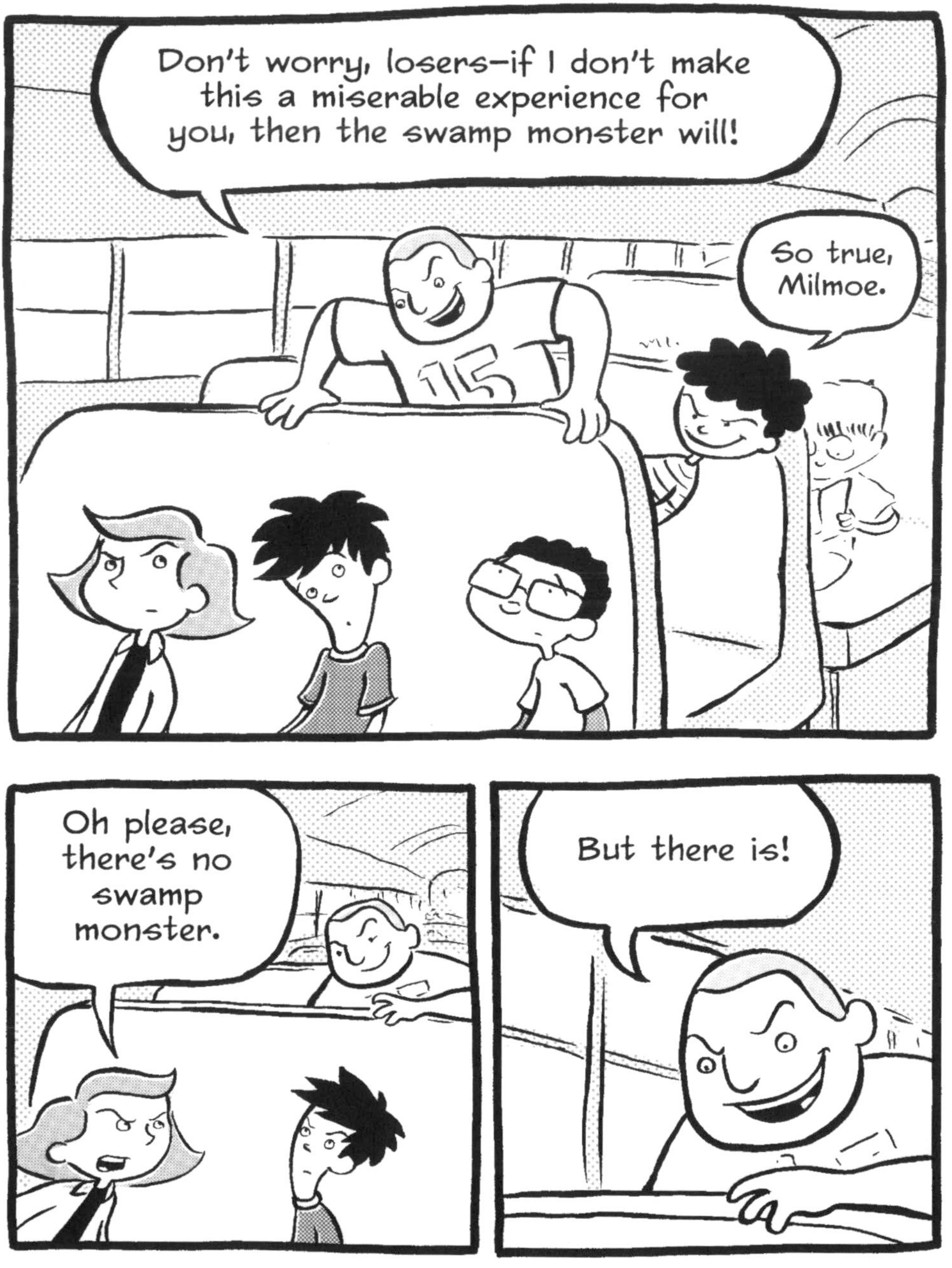
Don't worry, losers—if I don't make this a miserable experience for you, then the swamp monster will!
So true, Milmoe.
Oh please, there's no swamp monster.
But there is!

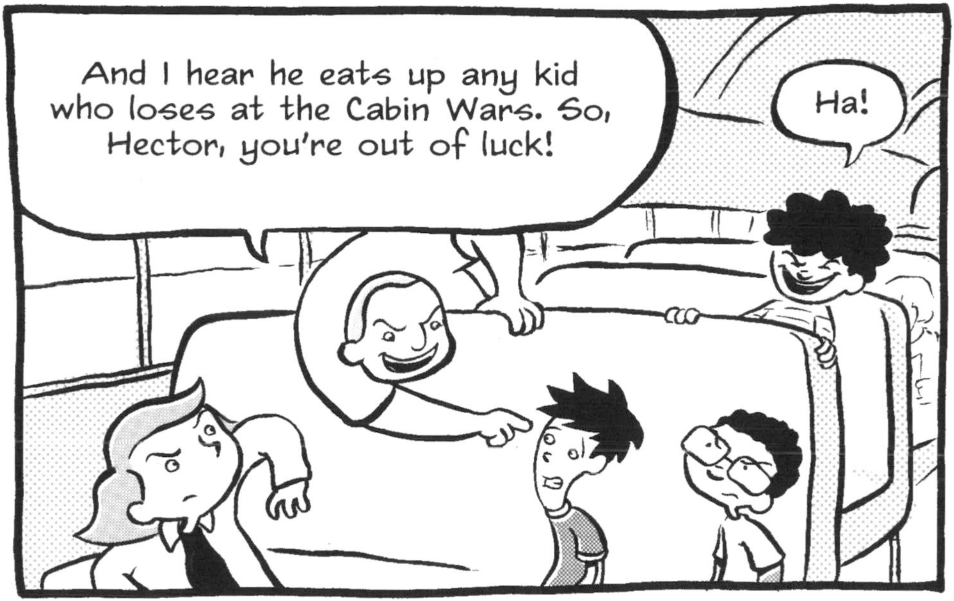
And I hear he eats up any kid who loses at the Cabin Wars. So, Hector, you're out of luck!
Ha!

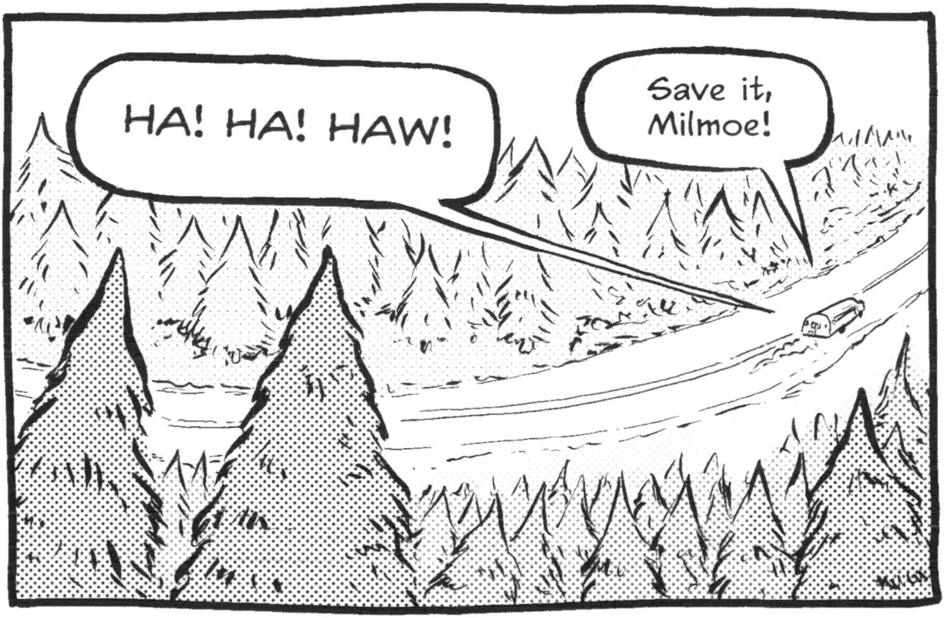
HA! HA! HAW!
Save it, Milmoe!

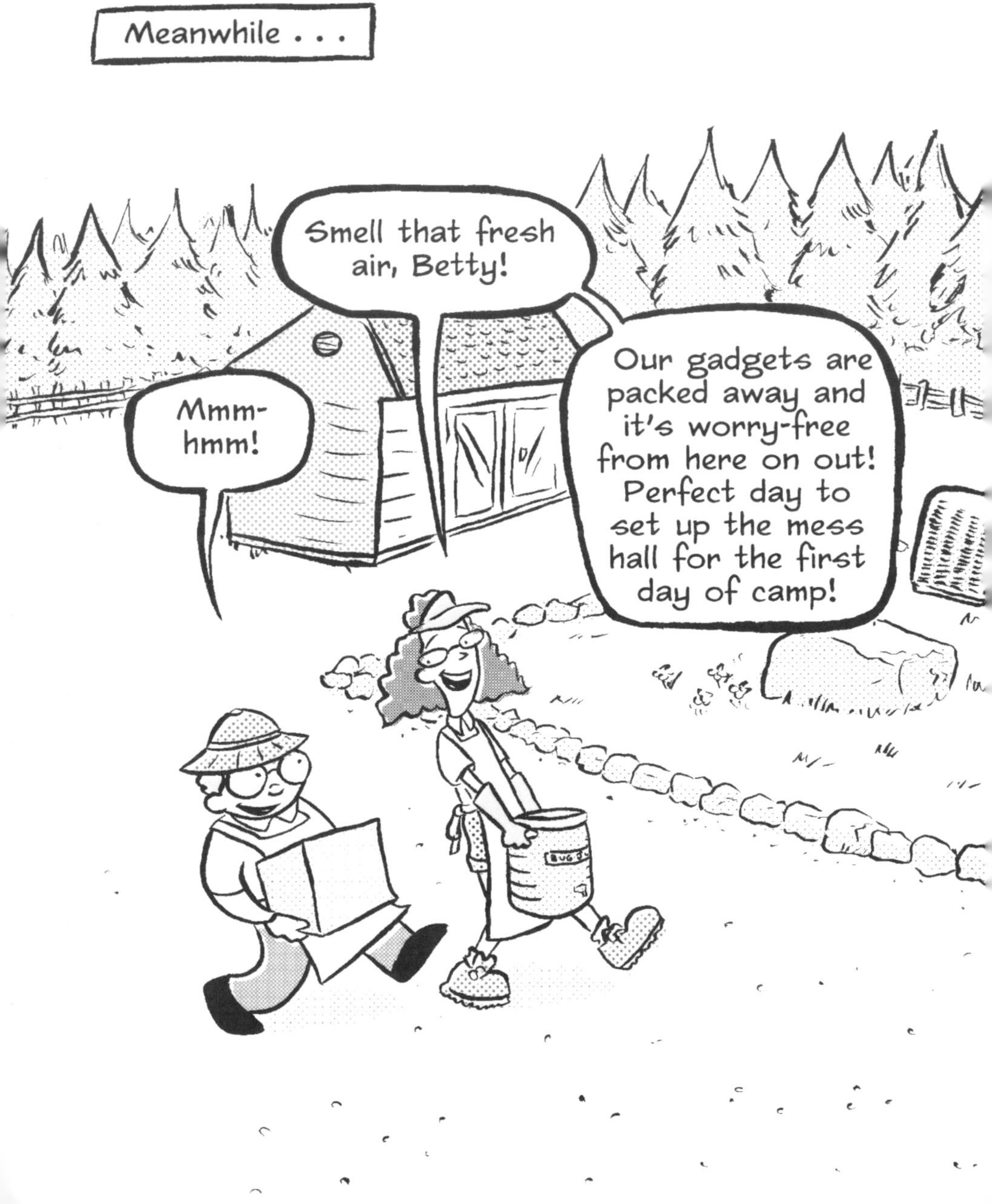
Meanwhile . . .
Smell that fresh air, Betty!
Mmm-hmm!
Our gadgets are packed away and it's worry-free from here on out! Perfect day to set up the mess hall for the first day of camp!

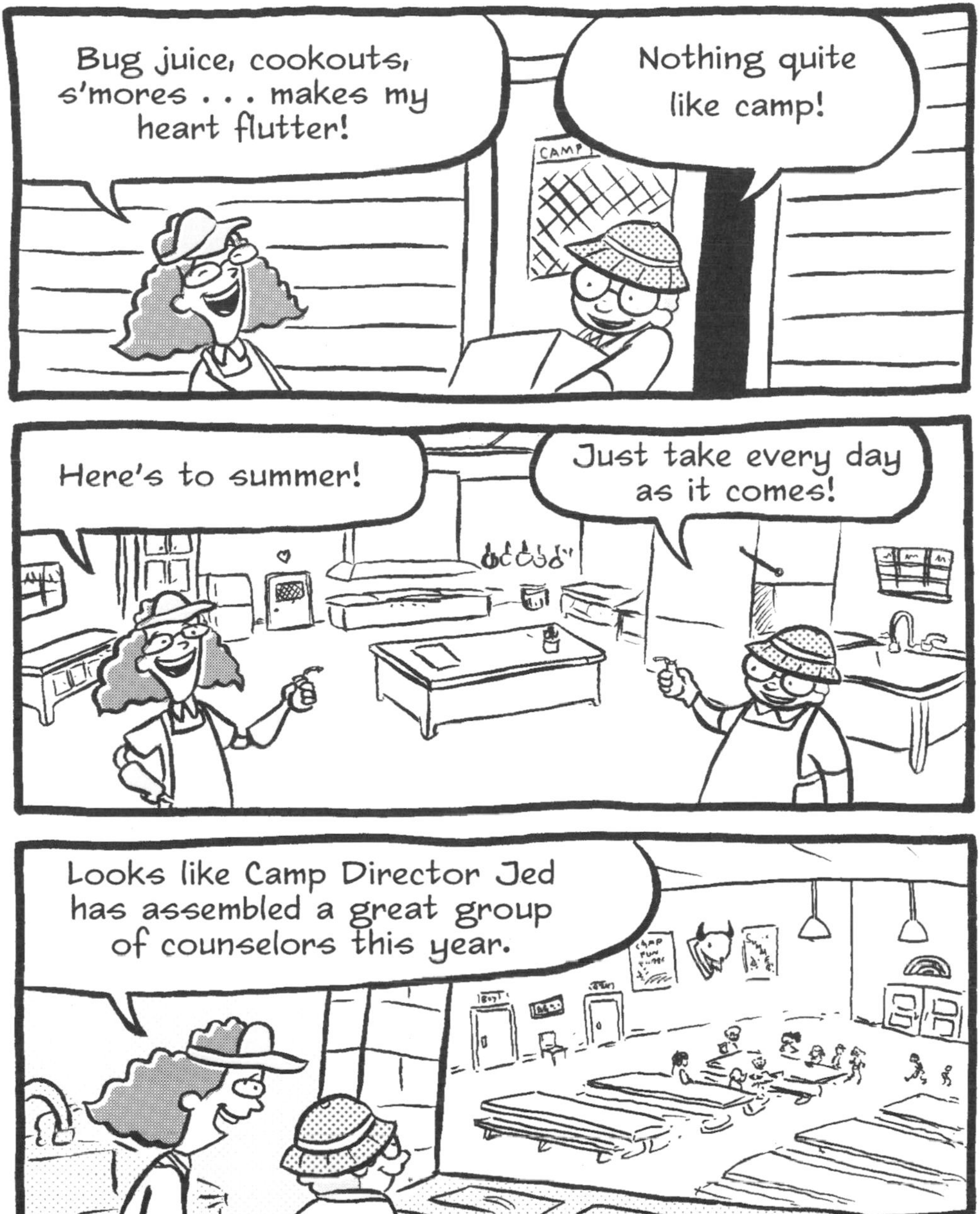
Bug juice, cookouts, s'mores . . . makes my heart flutter!
Nothing quite like camp!
CAMP
Here's to summer!
Just take every day as it comes!
Looks like Camp Director Jed has assembled a great group of counselors this year.

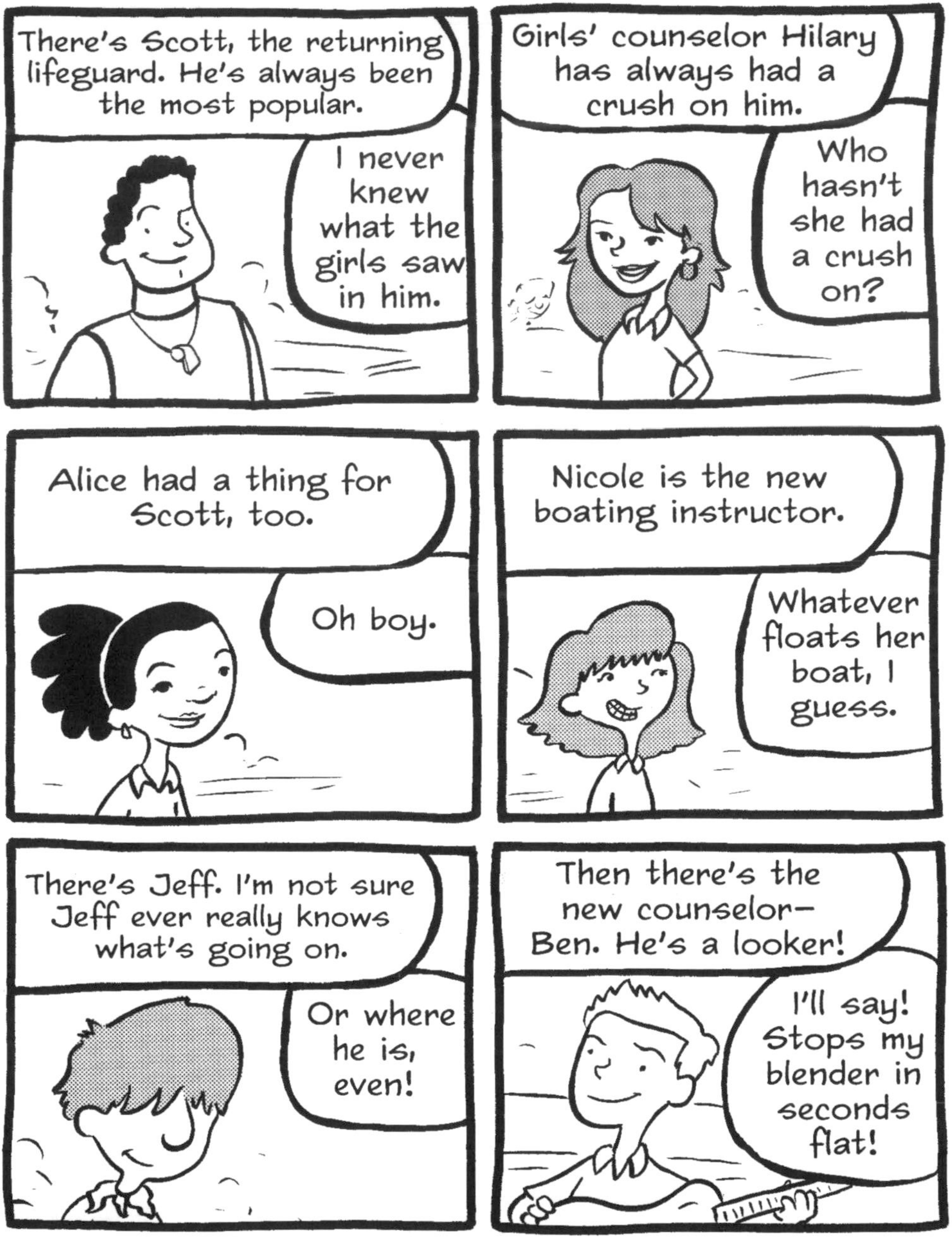
There's Scott, the returning lifeguard. He's always been the most popular.
I never knew what the girls saw in him.
Girls' counselor Hilary has always had a crush on him.
Who hasn't she had a crush on?
Alice had a thing for Scott, too.
Oh boy.
Nicole is the new boating instructor.
Whatever floats her boat, I guess.
There's Jeff. I'm not sure Jeff ever really knows what's going on.
Or where he is, even!
Then there's the new counselor—Ben. He's a looker!
I'll say! Stops my blender in seconds flat!

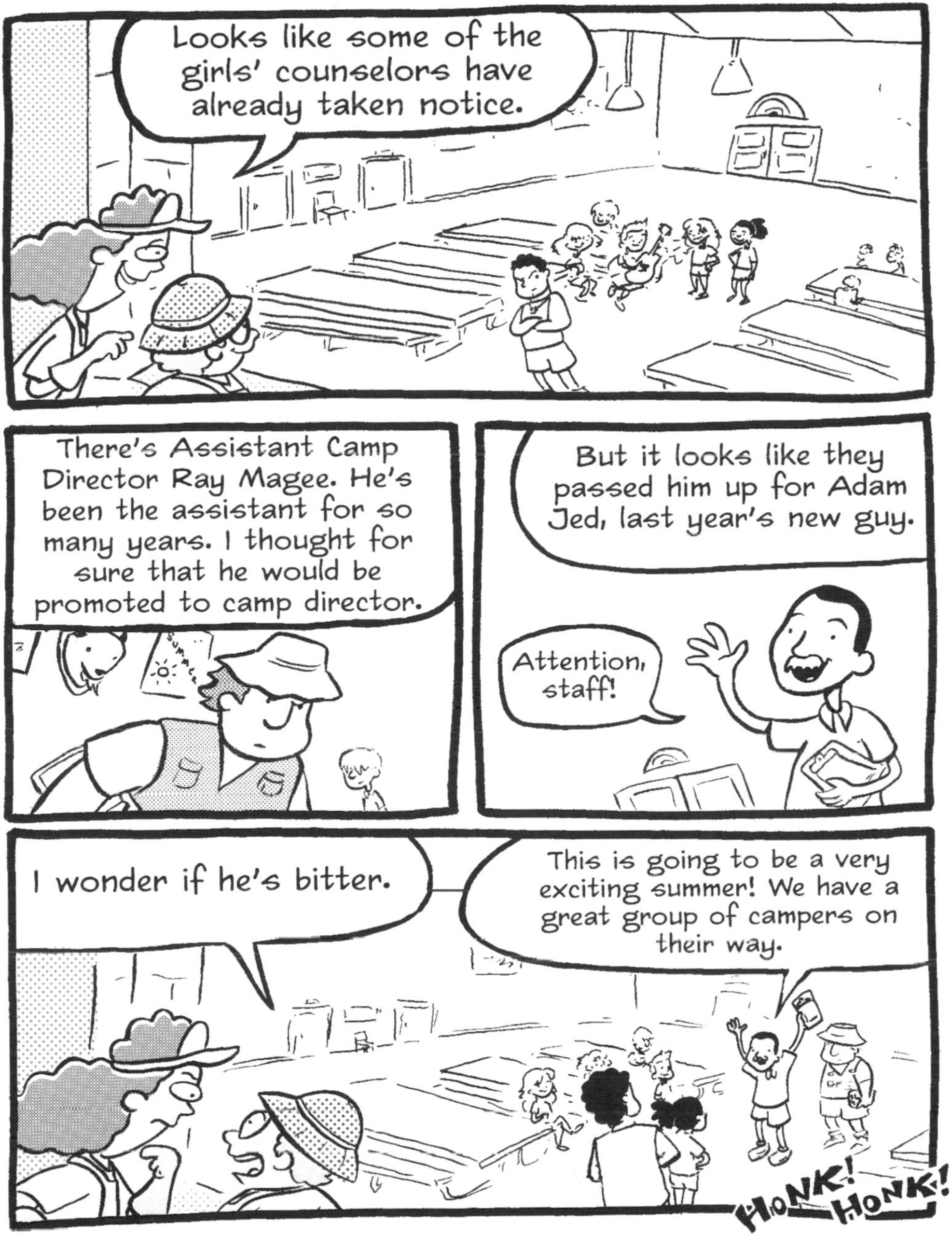
Looks like some of the girls' counselors have already taken notice.
There's Assistant Camp Director Ray Magee. He's been the assistant for so many years. I thought for sure that he would be promoted to camp director.
But it looks like they passed him up for Adam Jed, last year's new guy.
Attention, staff!
I wonder if he's bitter.
This is going to be a very exciting summer! We have a great group of campers on their way.
HONK! HONK!

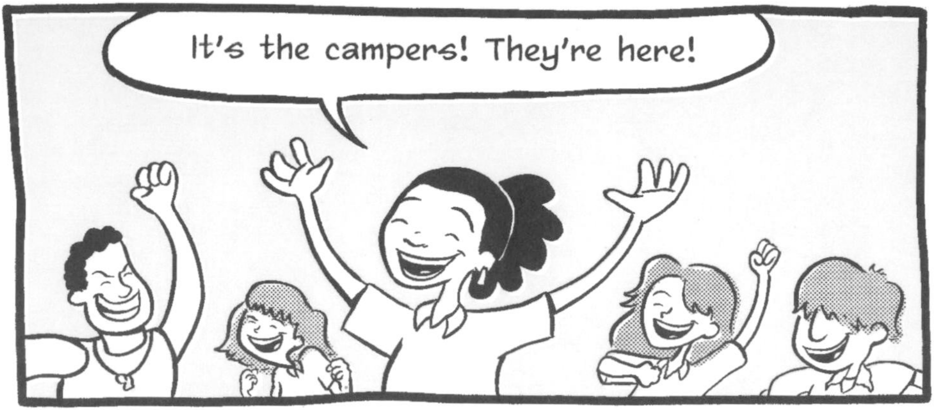
It's the campers! They're here!

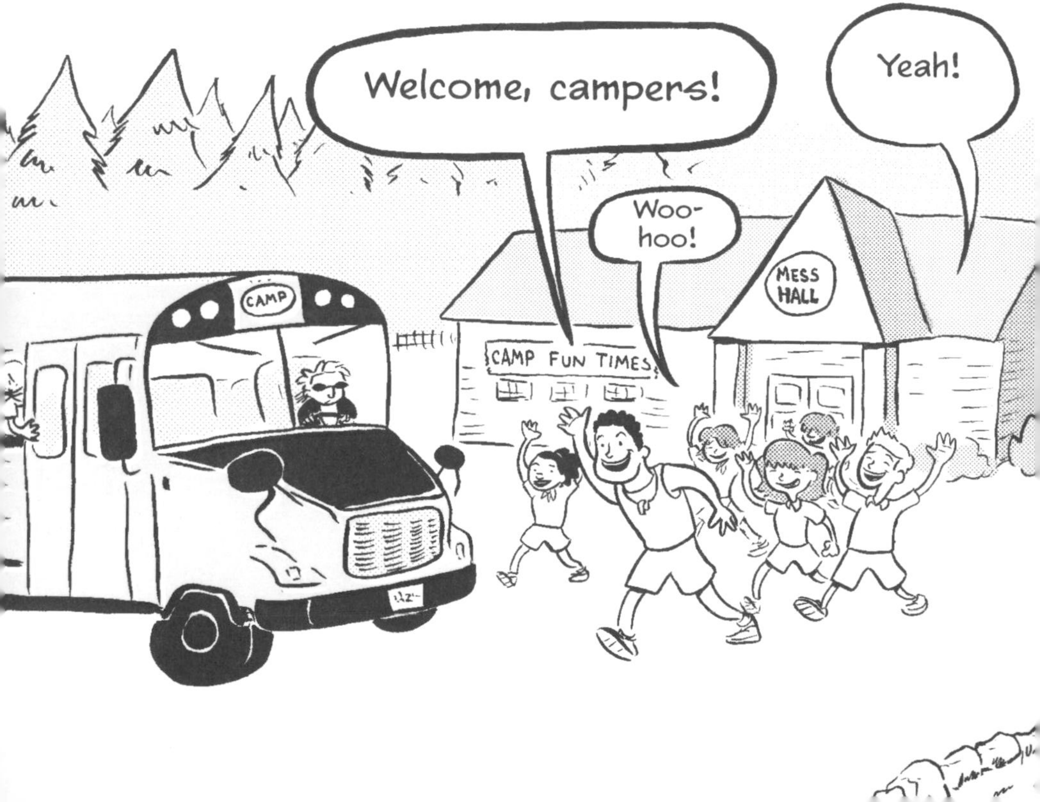
Welcome, campers!
Woo-hoo!
Yeah!
CAMP
CAMP FUN TIMES
MESS HALL

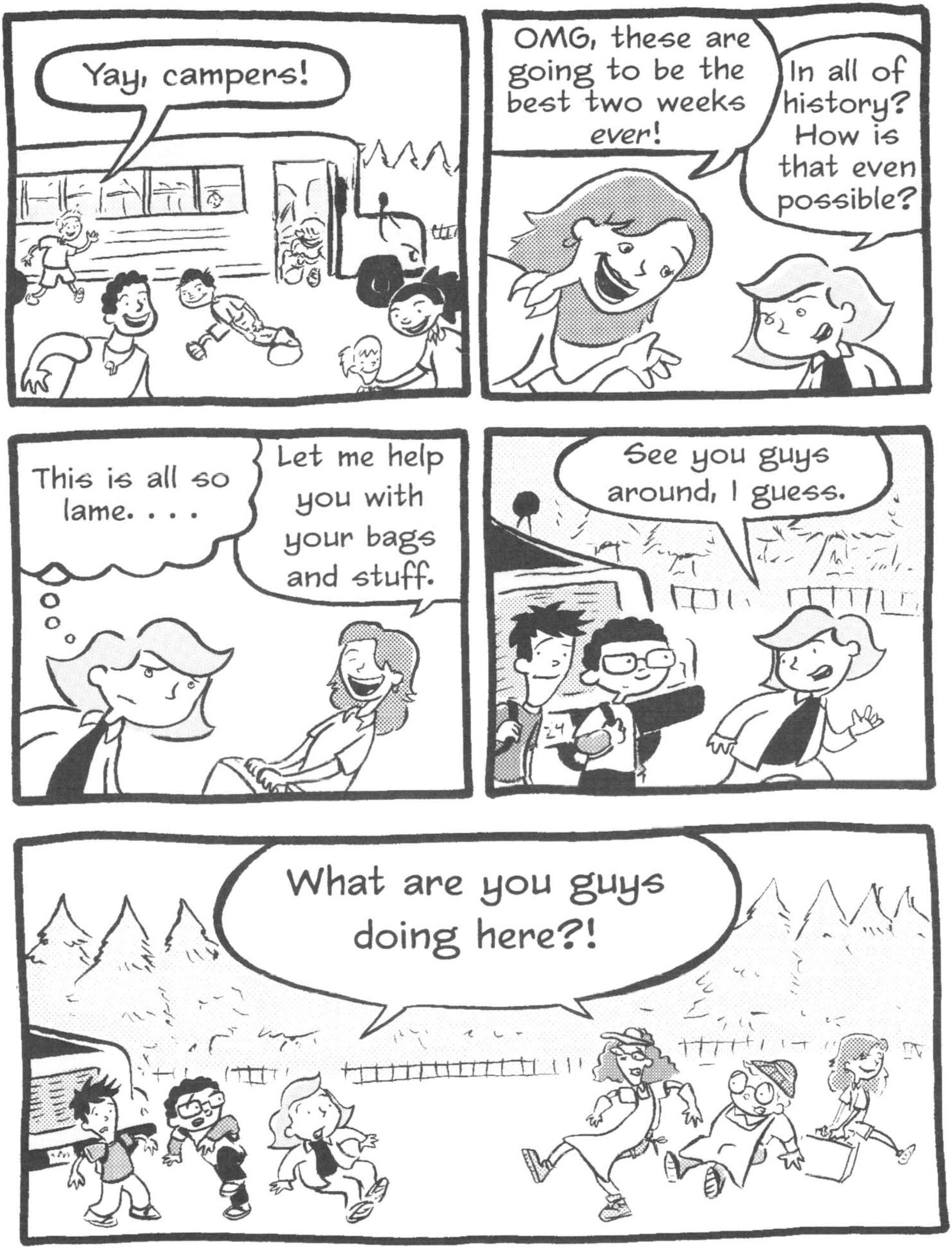

Yay, campers!
OMG, these are going to be the best two weeks ever!
In all of history? How is that even possible?
This is all so lame. . . .
Let me help you with your bags and stuff.
See you guys around, I guess.
What are you guys doing here?!

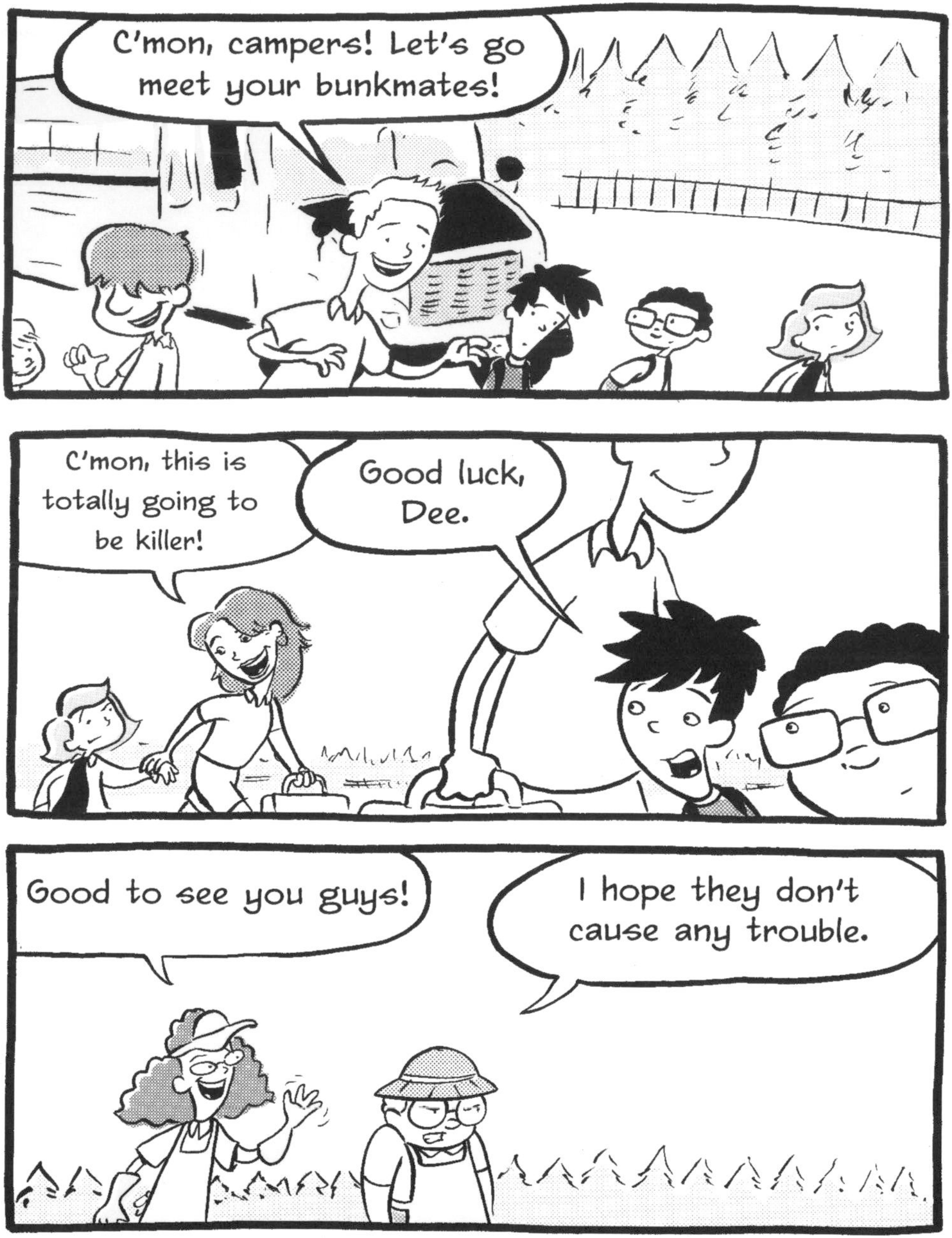
C'mon, campers! Let's go meet your bunkmates!
C'mon, this is totally going to be killer!
Good luck, Dee.
Good to see you guys!
I hope they don't cause any trouble.

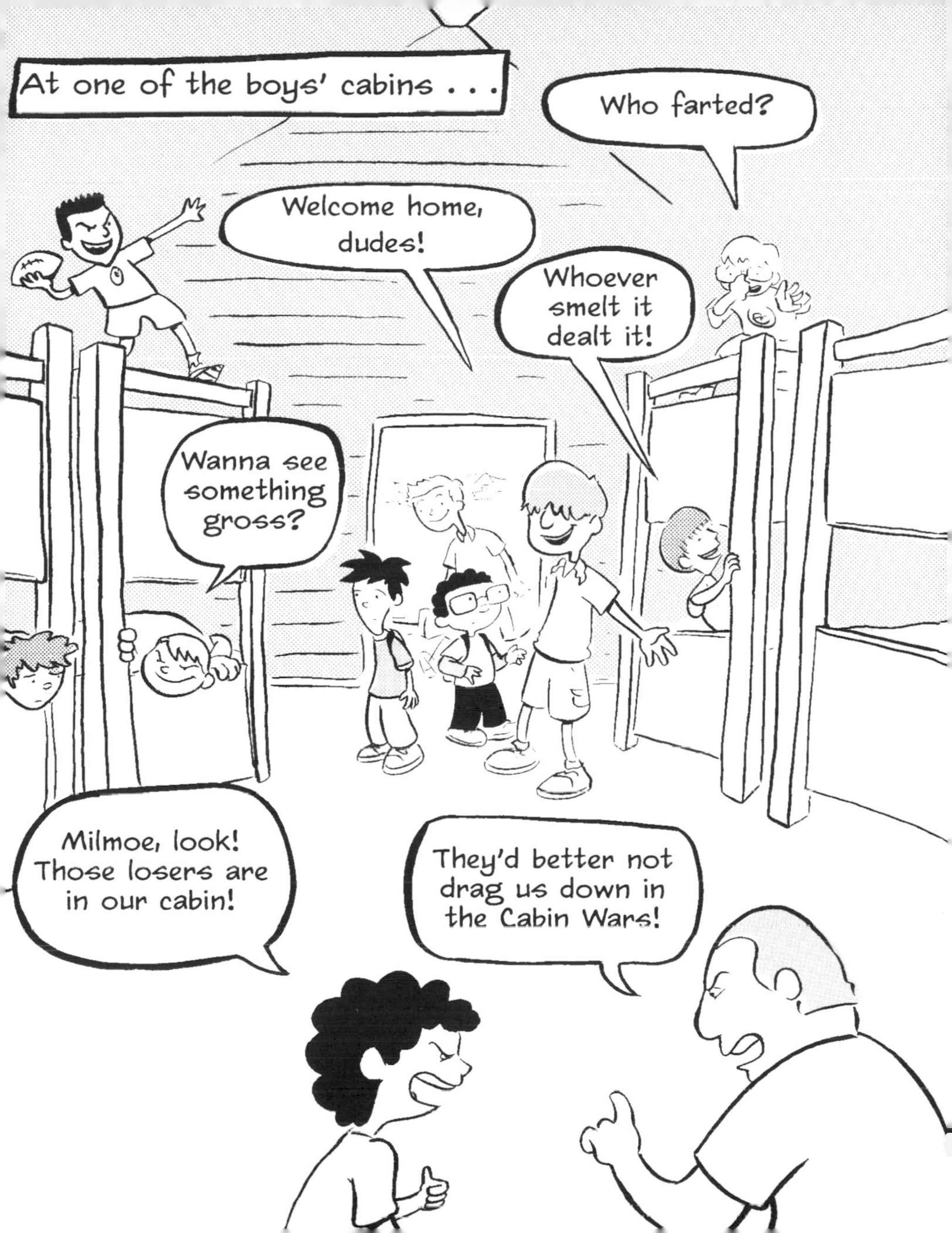
At one of the boys' cabins . . .
Who farted?
Welcome home, dudes!
Whoever smelt it dealt it!
Wanna see something gross?
Milmoe, look! Those losers are in our cabin!
They'd better not drag us down in the Cabin Wars!

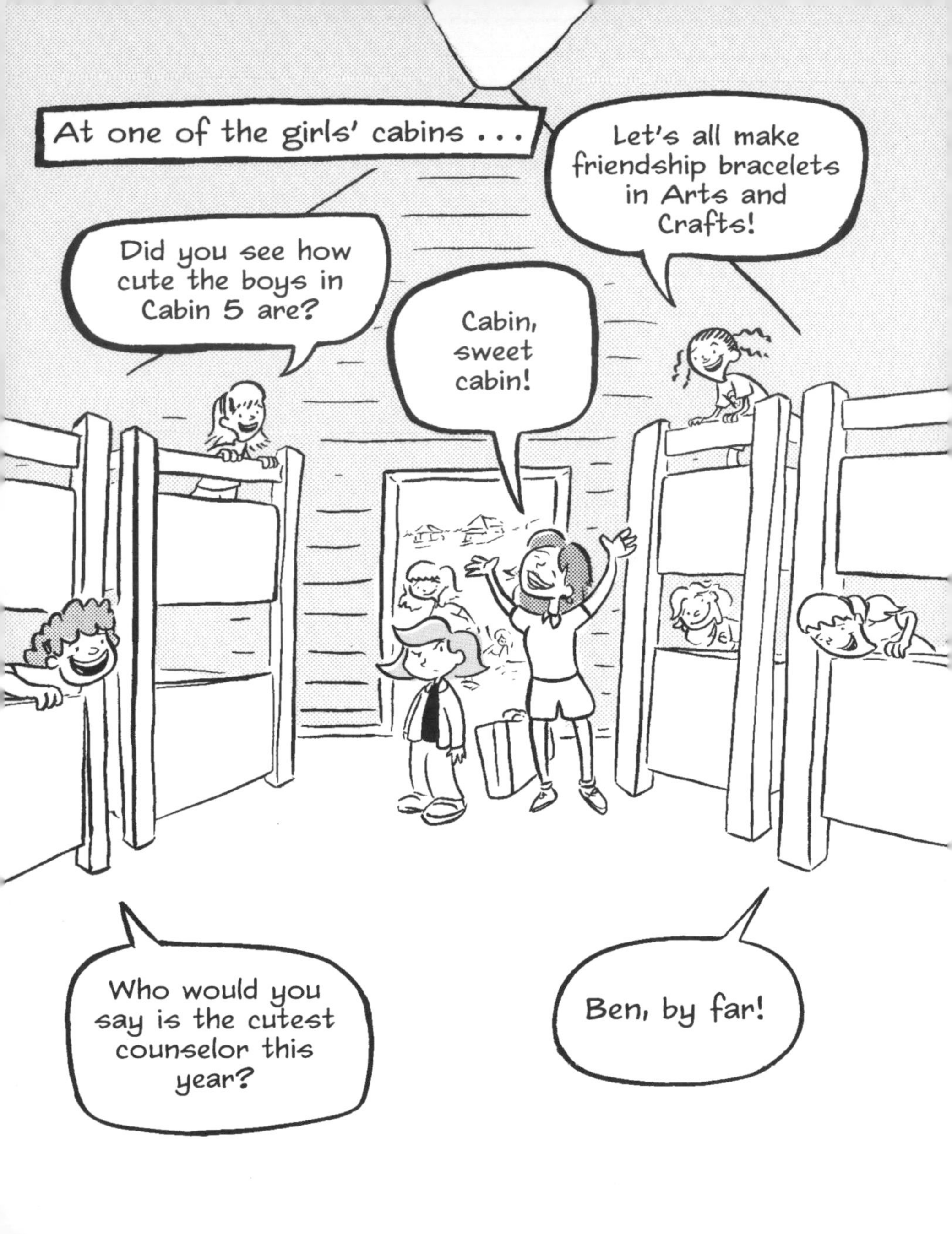
At one of the girls' cabins . . .
Let's all make friendship bracelets in Arts and Crafts!
Did you see how cute the boys in Cabin 5 are?
Cabin, sweet cabin!
Who would you say is the cutest counselor this year?
Ben, by far!

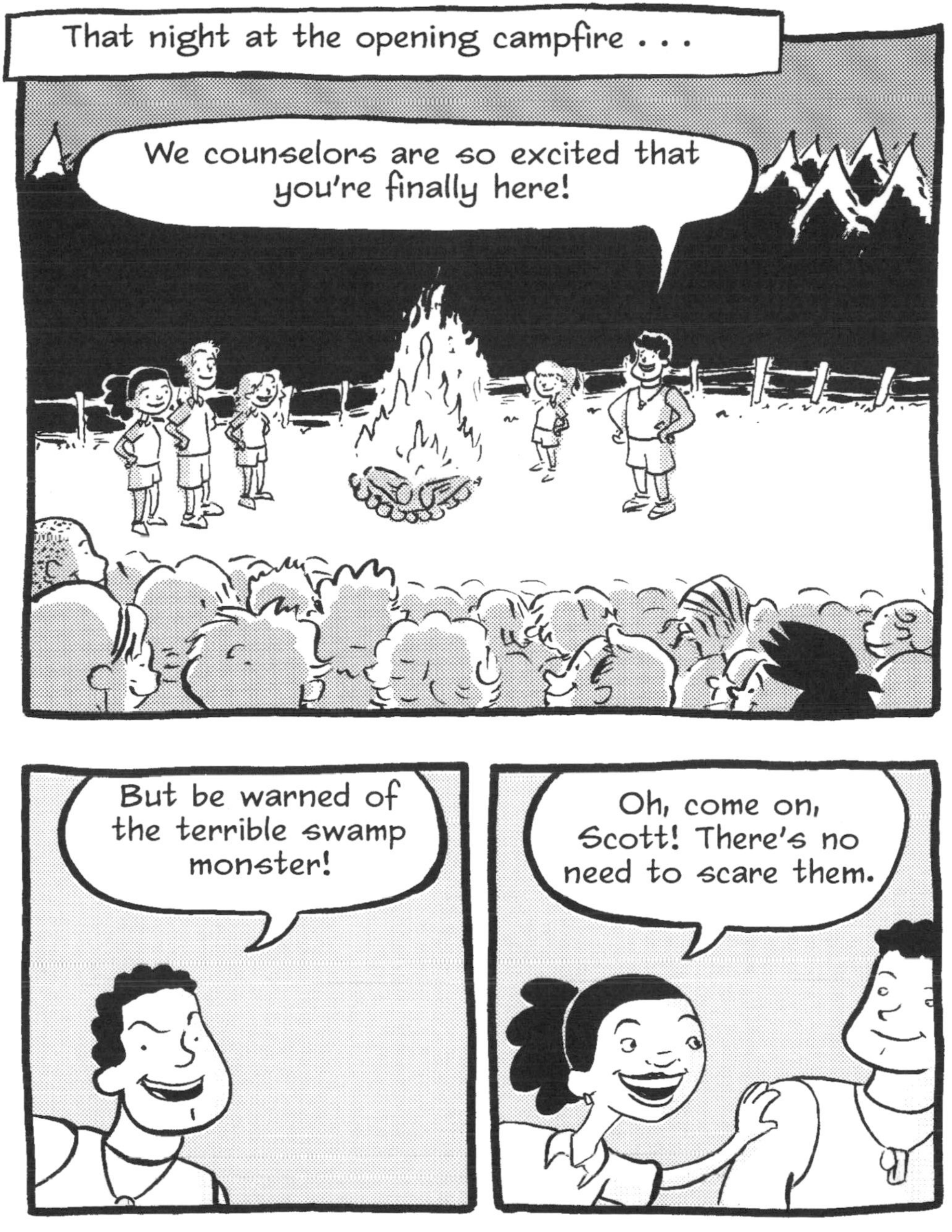
That night at the opening campfire . . .
We counselors are so excited that you're finally here!
But be warned of the terrible swamp monster!
Oh, come on, Scott! There's no need to scare them.

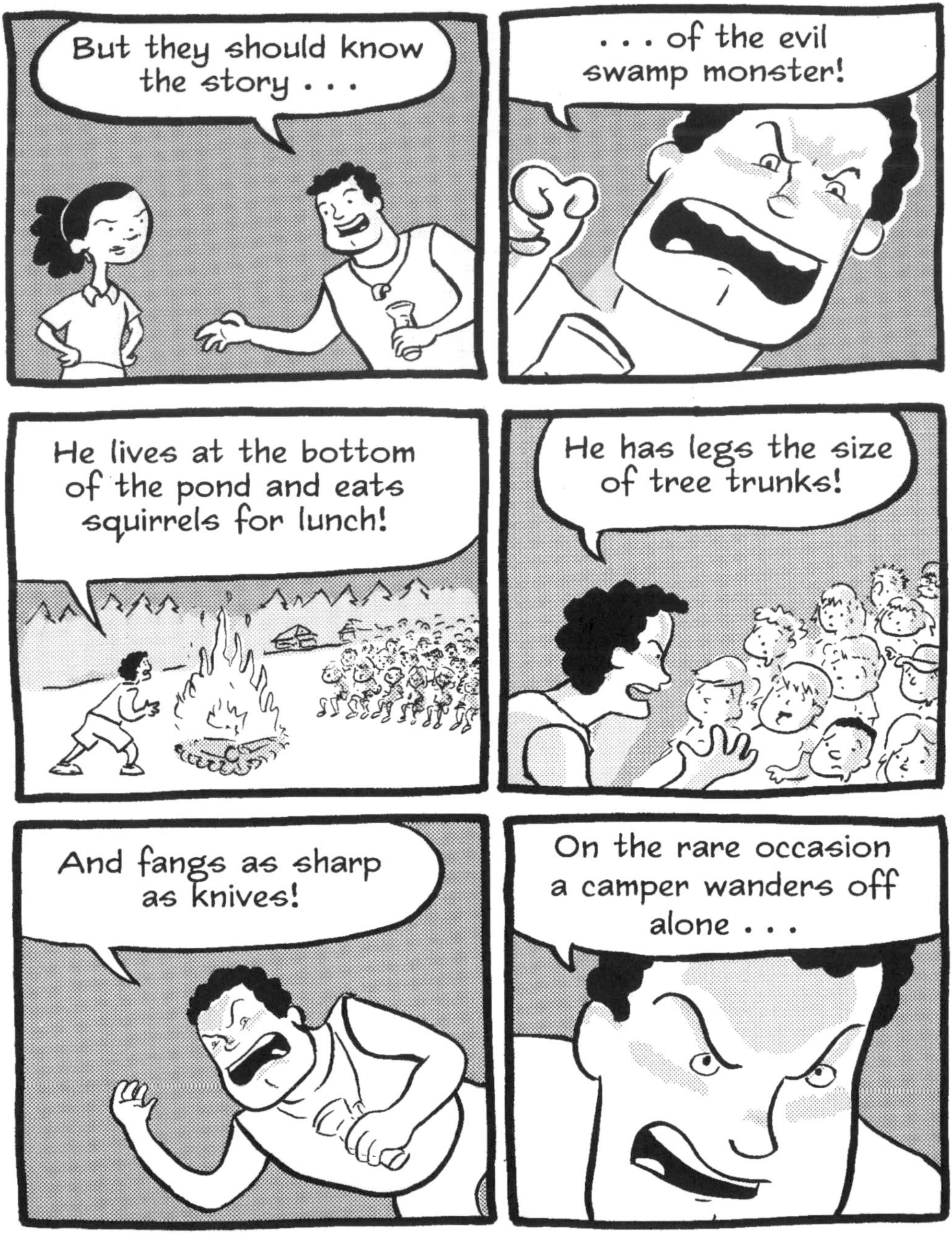
But they should know the story . . .
. . . of the evil swamp monster!
He lives at the bottom of the pond and eats squirrels for lunch!
He has legs the size of tree trunks!
And fangs as sharp as knives!
On the rare occasion a camper wanders off alone . . .

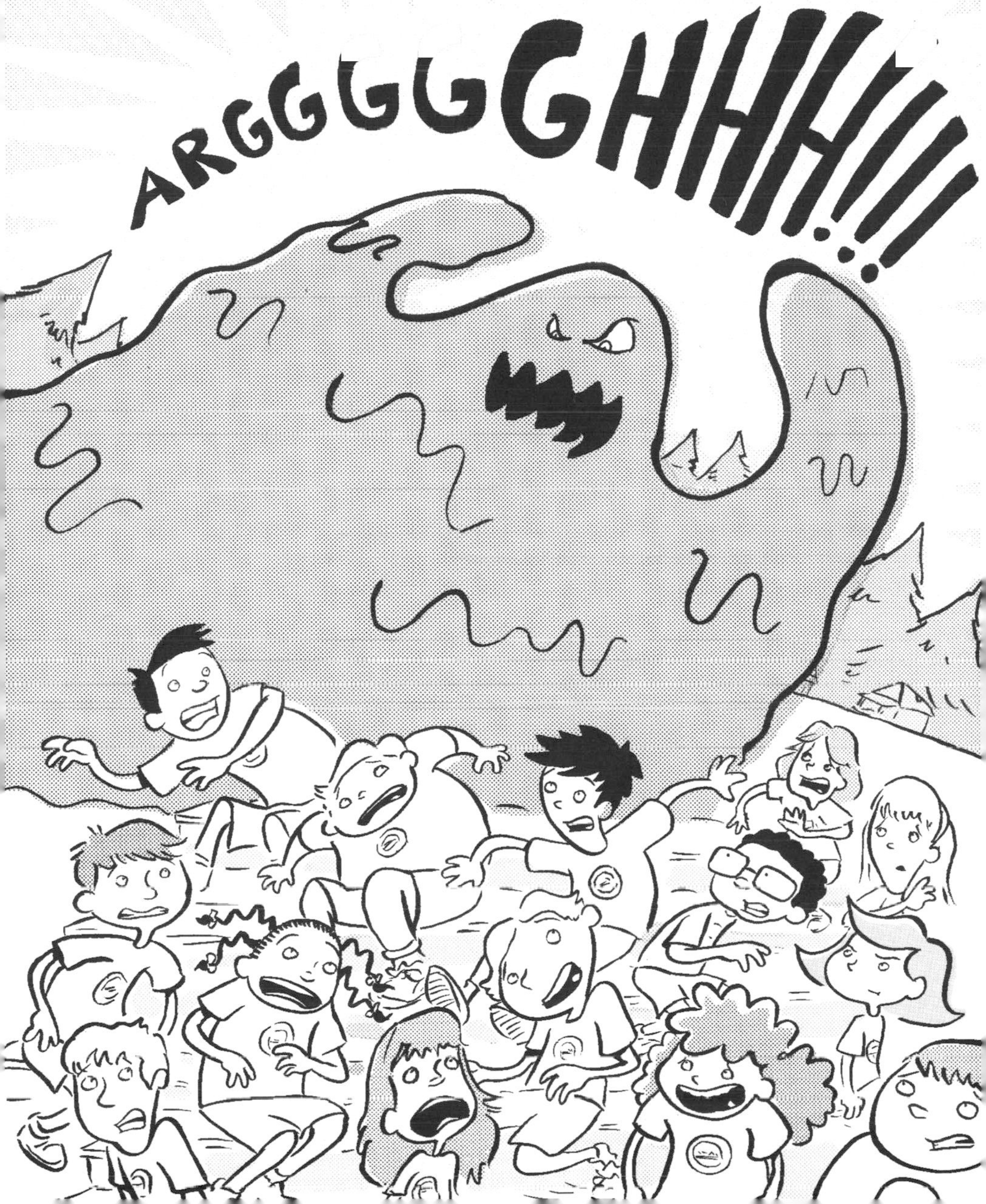
ARGGGGGGHHHH!!!

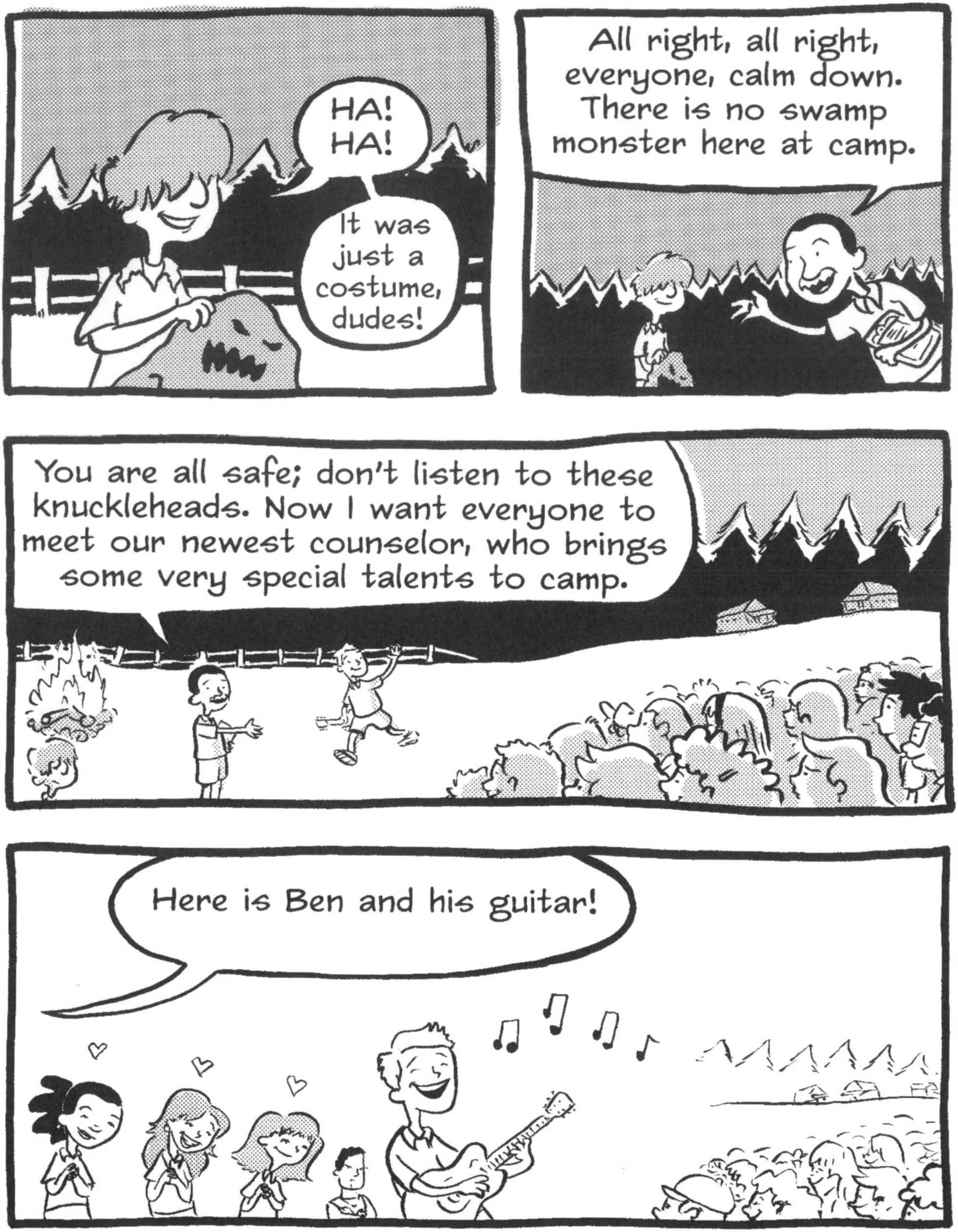
HA! HA!
It was just a costume, dudes!
All right, all right, everyone, calm down. There is no swamp monster here at camp.
You are all safe; don't listen to these knuckleheads. Now I want everyone to meet our newest counselor, who brings some very special talents to camp.
Here is Ben and his guitar!

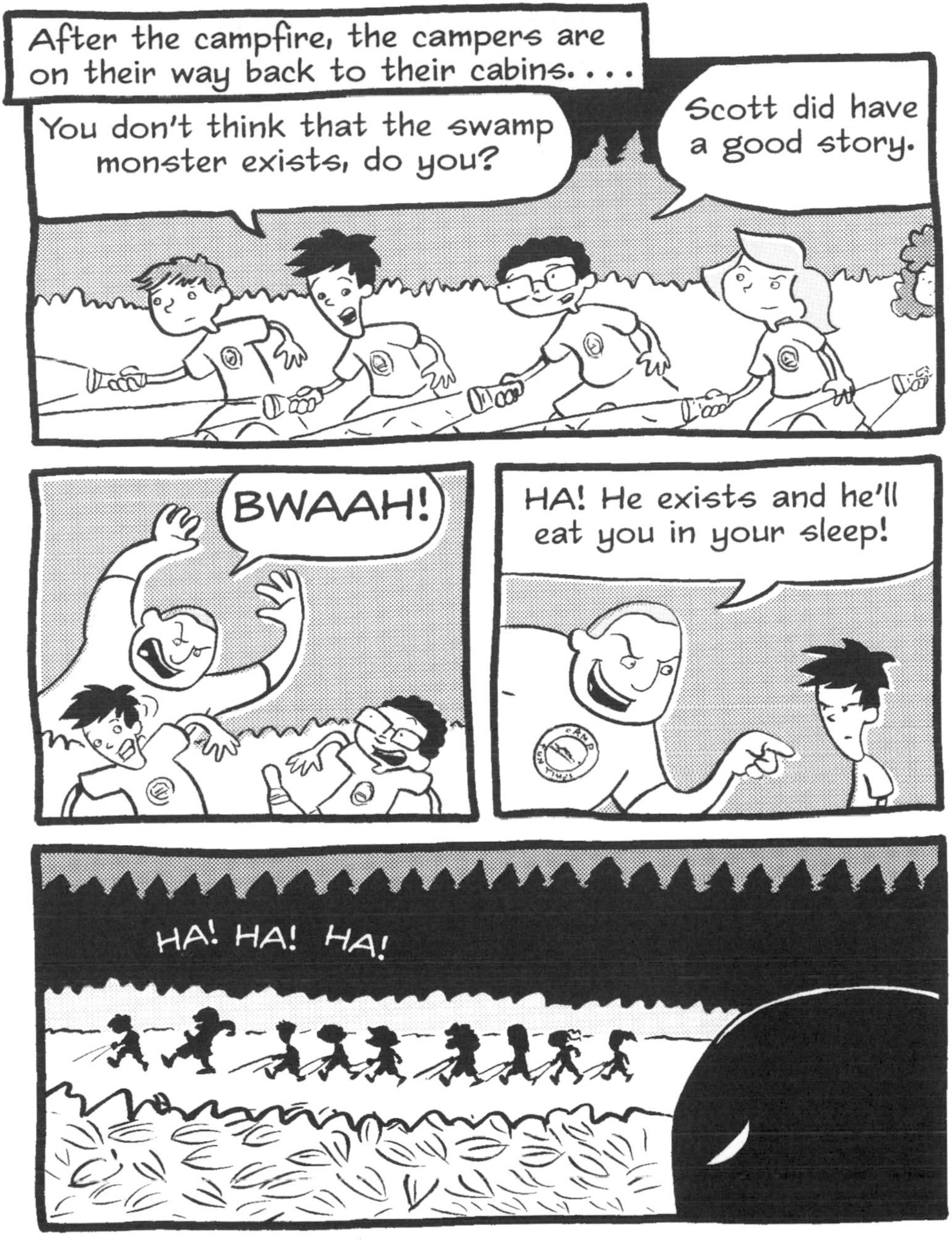
After the campfire, the campers are on their way back to their cabins. . . .
You don't think that the swamp monster exists, do you?
Scott did have a good story.
BWAAH!
HA! He exists and he'll eat you in your sleep!
HA! HA! HA!

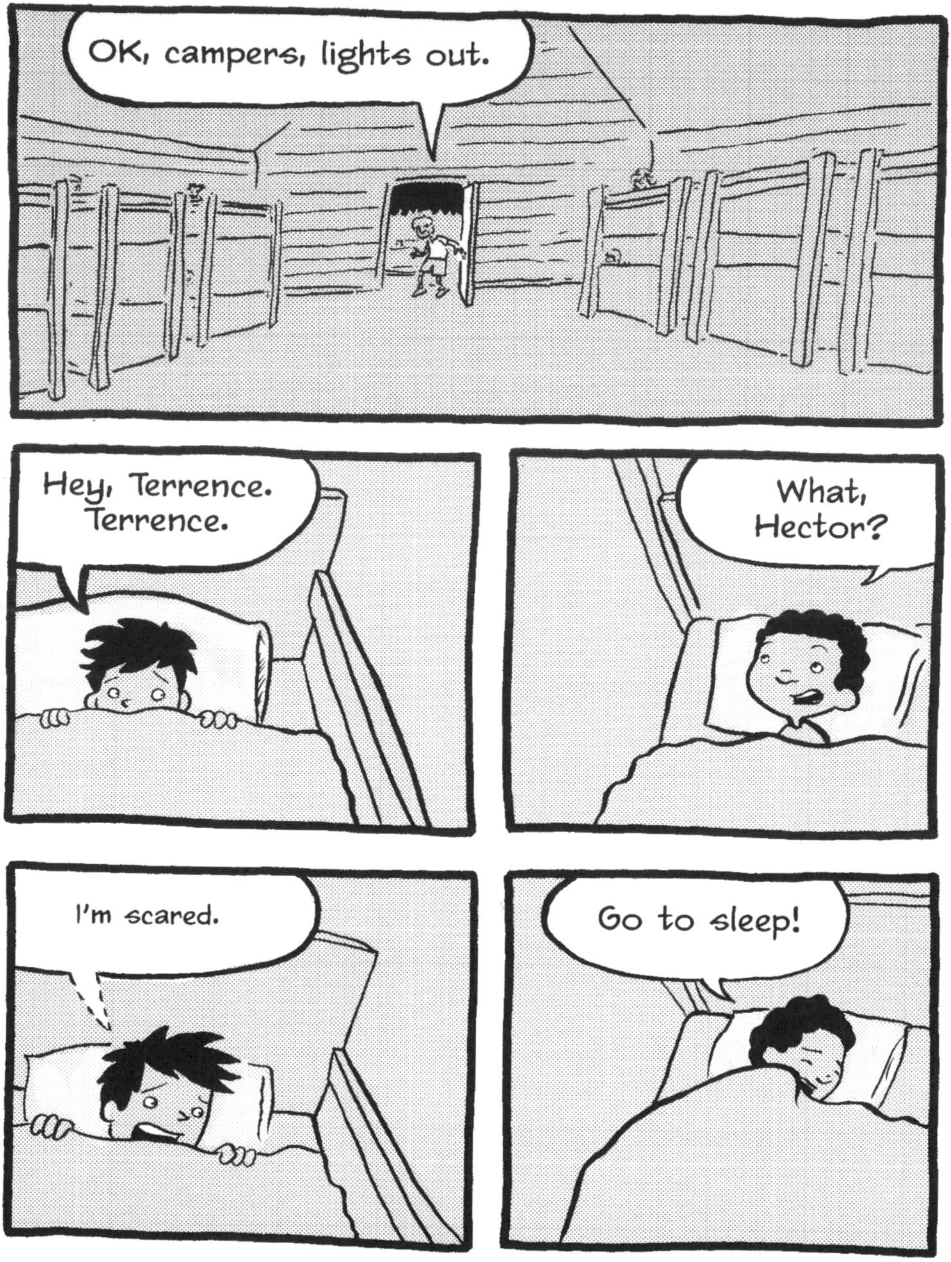
OK, campers, lights out.
Hey, Terrence. Terrence.
What, Hector?
I'm scared.
Go to sleep!

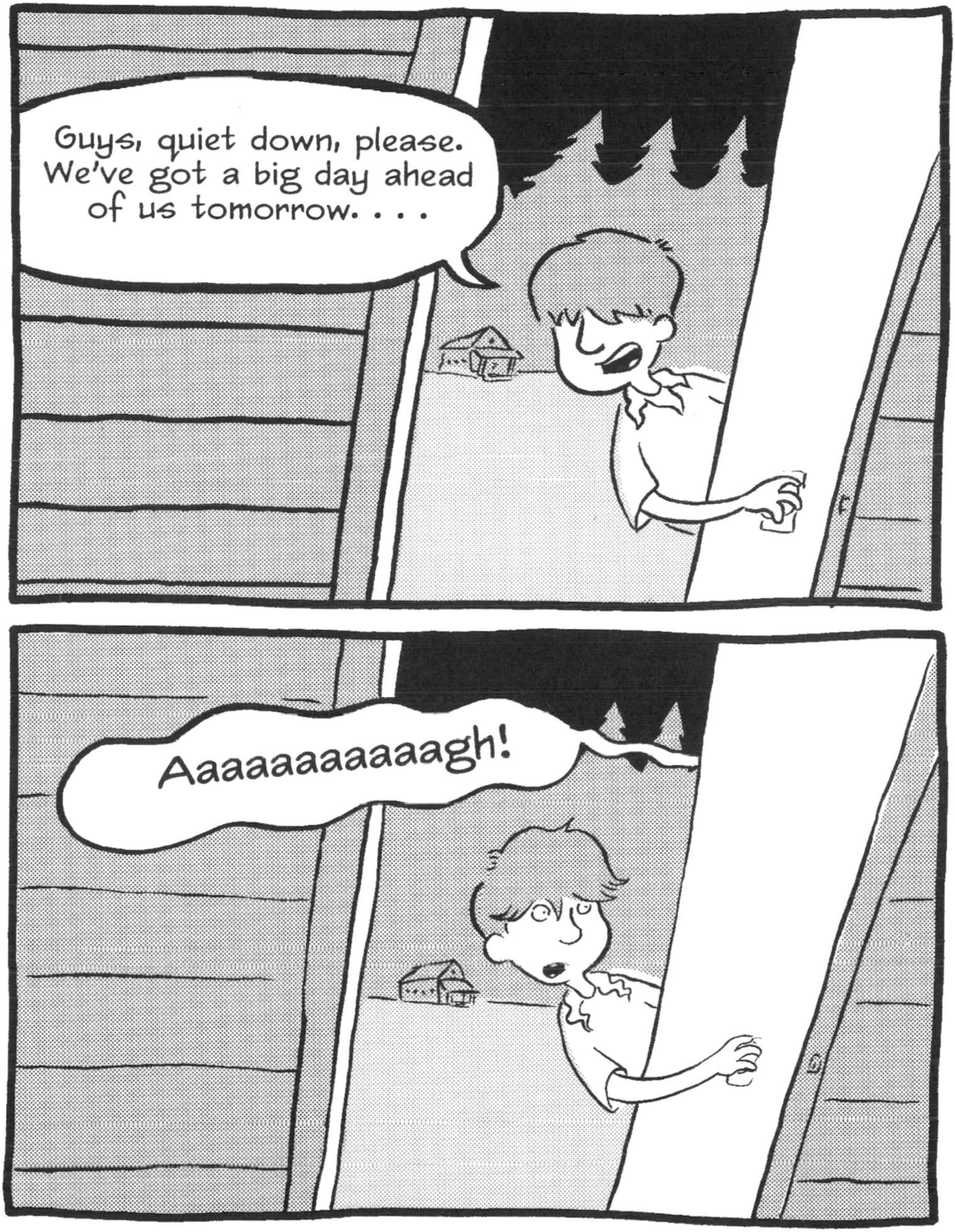
Guys, quiet down, please. We've got a big day ahead of us tomorrow. . . .
Aaaaaaaaaaagh!

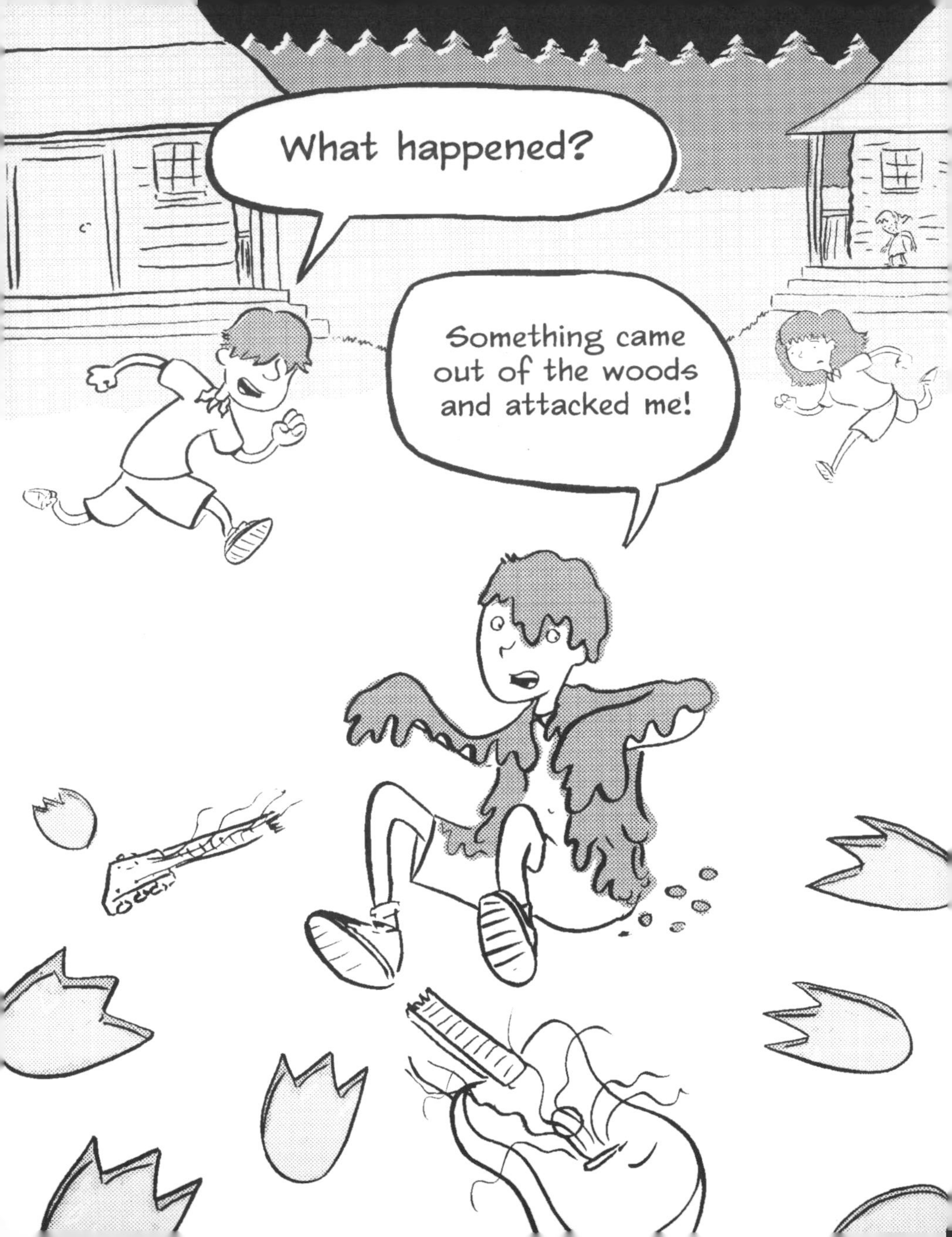
What happened?
Something came out of the woods and attacked me!

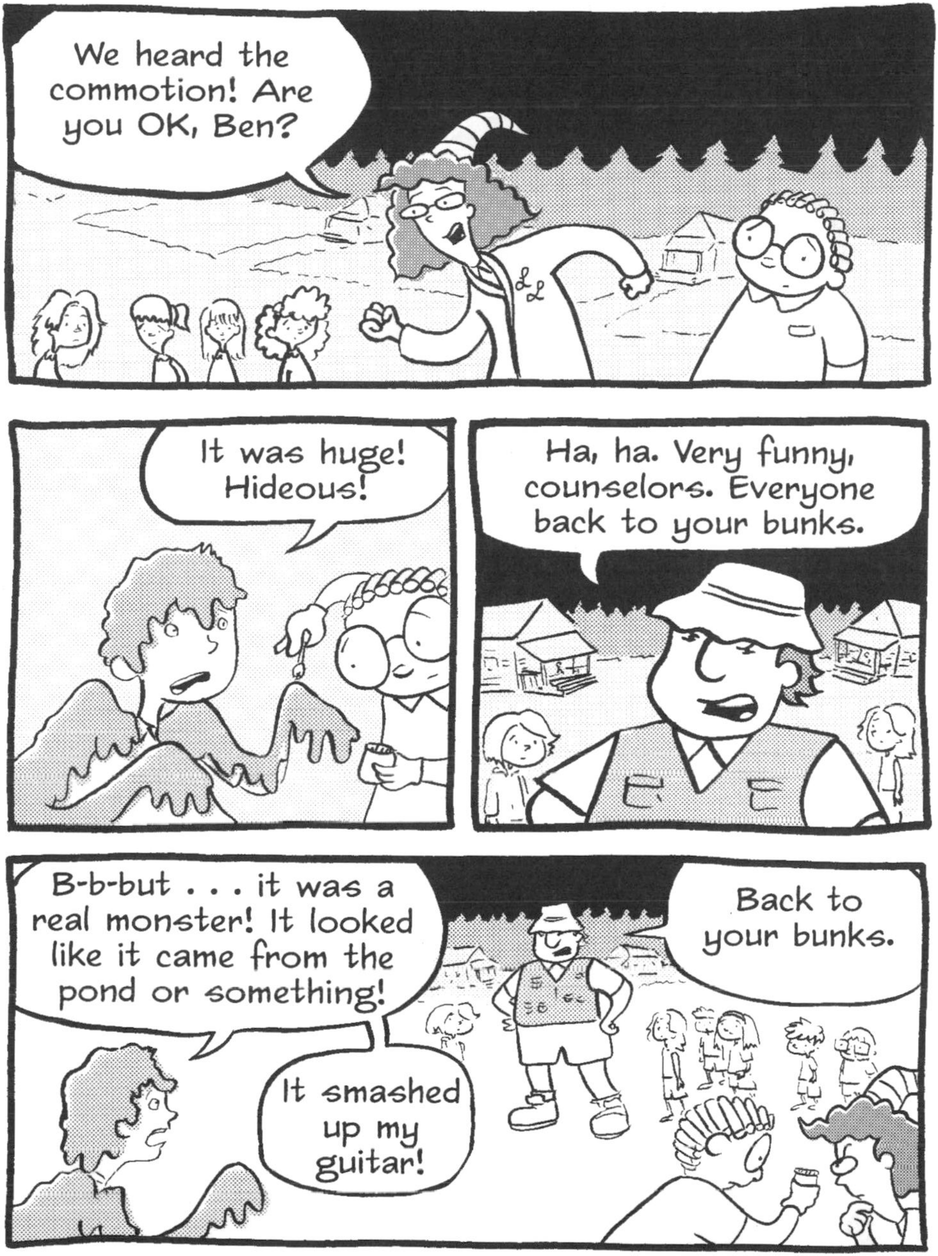

We heard the commotion! Are you OK, Ben?
It was huge! Hideous!
Ha, ha. Very funny, counselors. Everyone back to your bunks.
B-b-but . . . it was a real monster! It looked like it came from the pond or something!
Back to your bunks.
It smashed up my guitar!

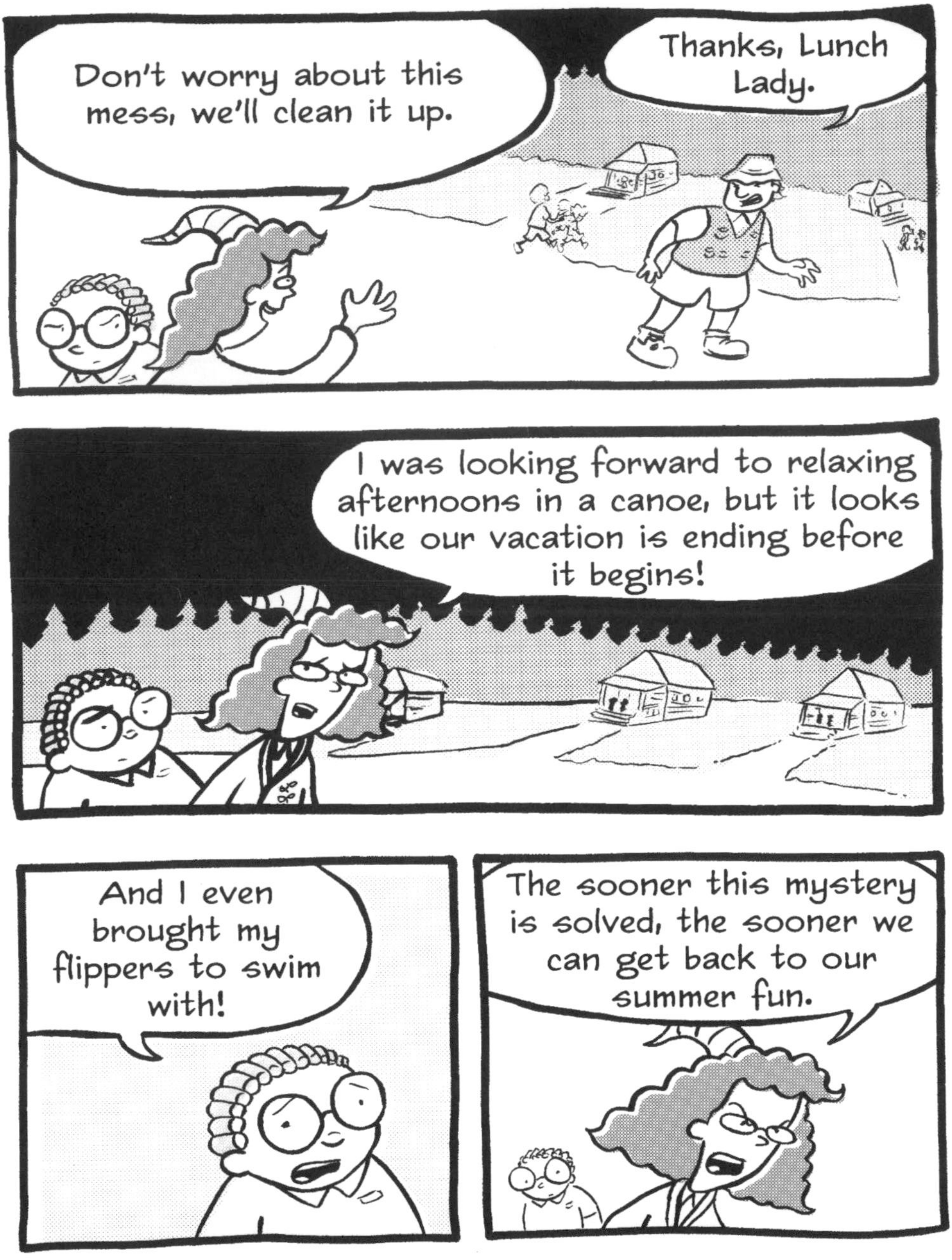
Don't worry about this mess, we'll clean it up.
Thanks, Lunch Lady.
I was looking forward to relaxing afternoons in a canoe, but it looks like our vacation is ending before it begins!
And I even brought my flippers to swim with!
The sooner this mystery is solved, the sooner we can get back to our summer fun.

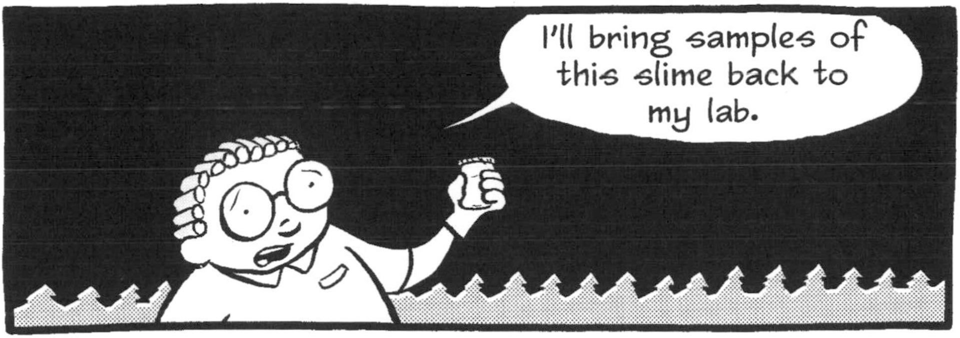
I'll bring samples of this slime back to my lab.

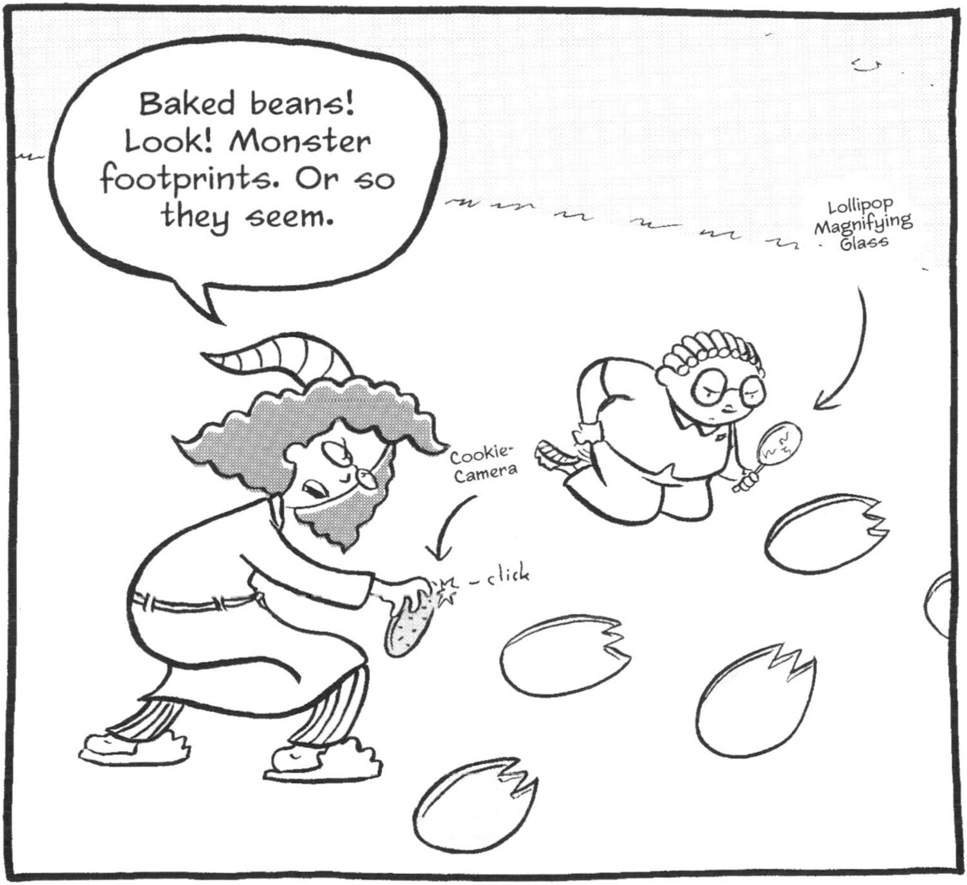
Baked beans! Look! Monster footprints. Or so they seem.
Lollipop Magnifying Glass
Cookie-Camera
click

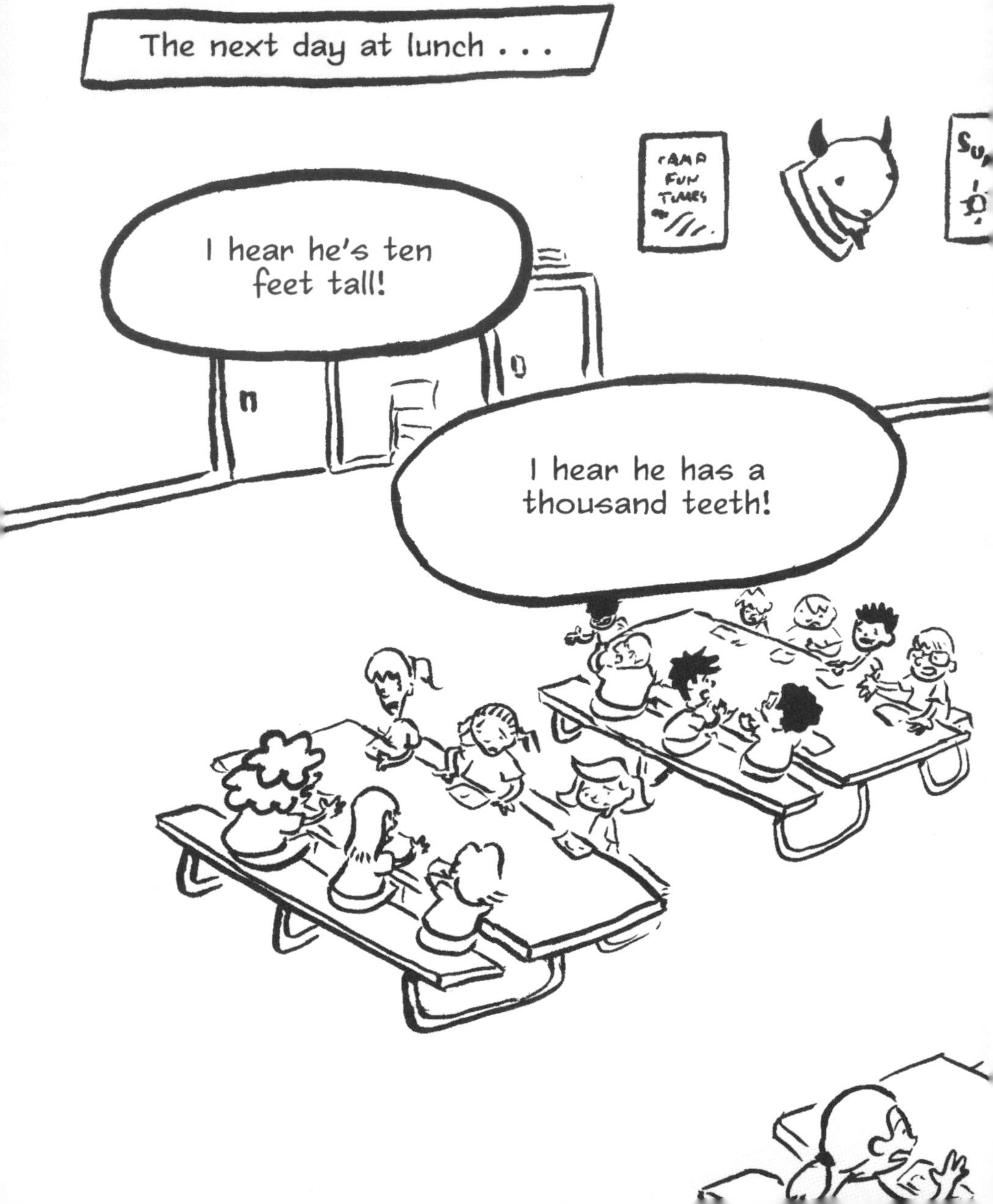

The next day at lunch . . .
CAMP FUN TIMES
I hear he's ten feet tall!
I hear he has a thousand teeth!

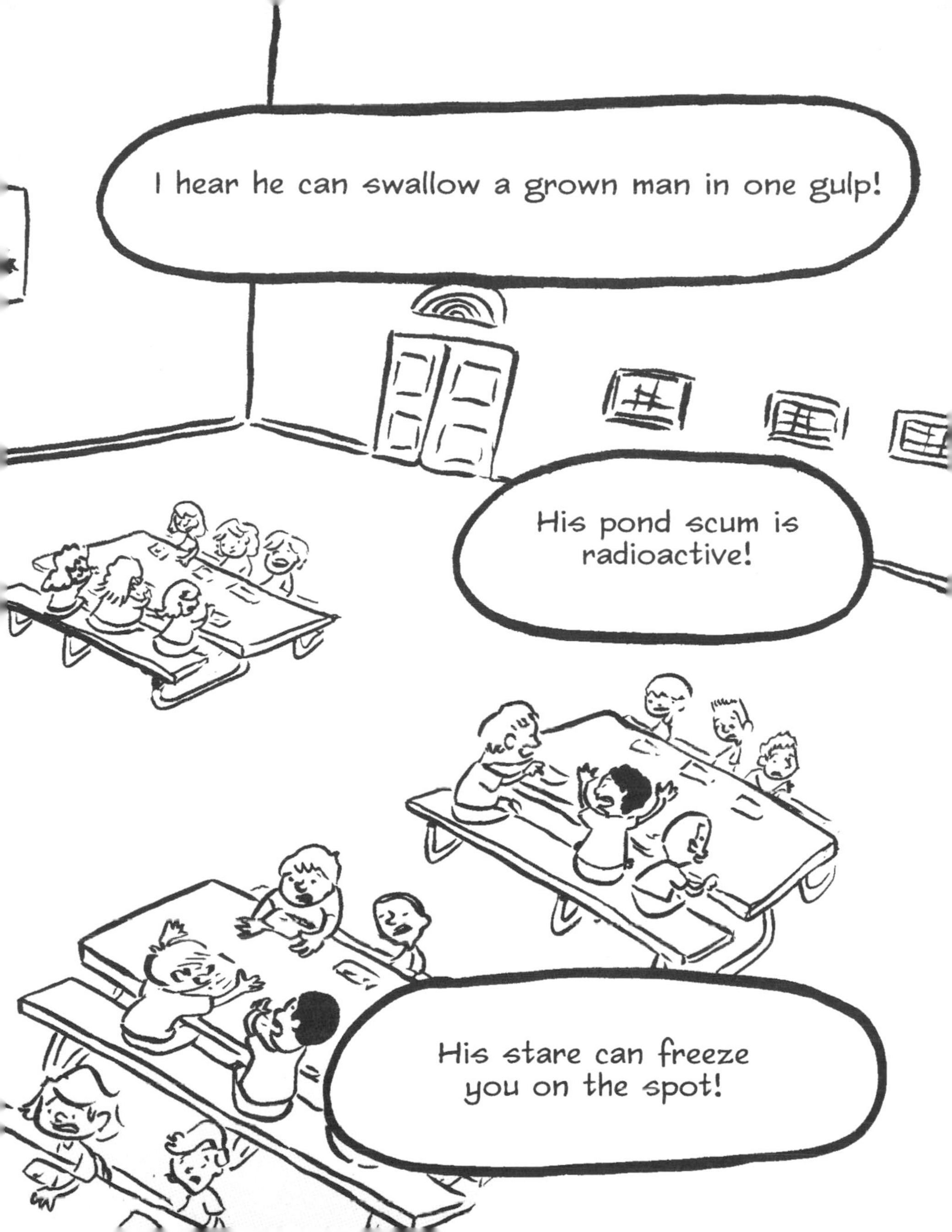
I hear he can swallow a grown man in one gulp!
His pond scum is radioactive!
His stare can freeze you on the spot!

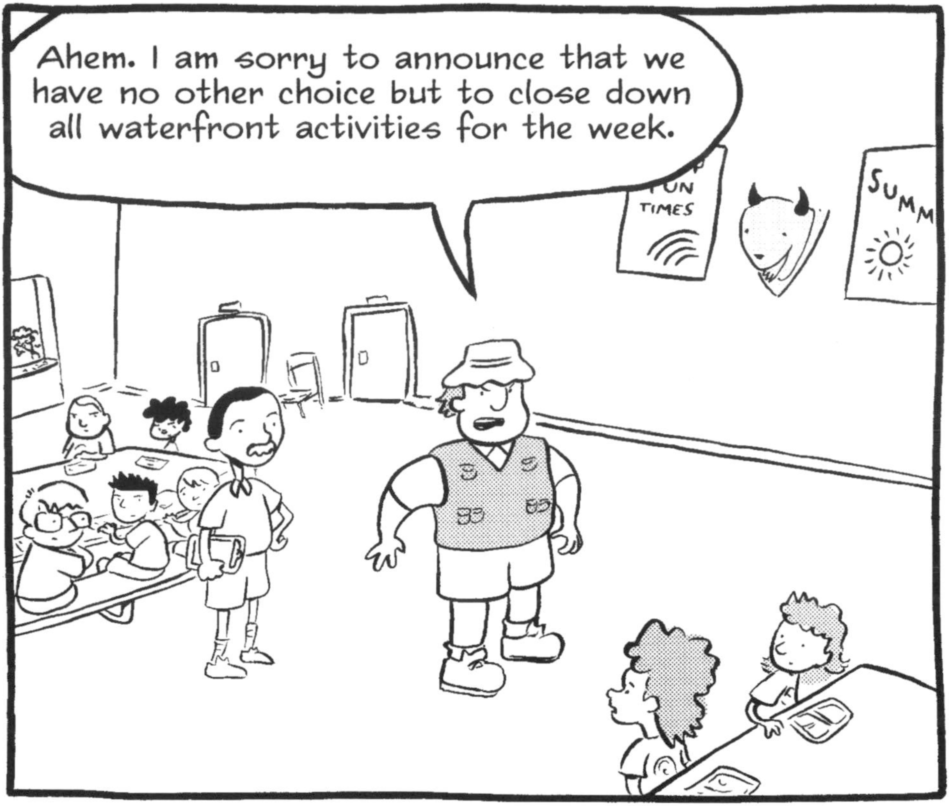
Ahem. I am sorry to announce that we have no other choice but to close down all waterfront activities for the week.
FUN TIMES
SUMM

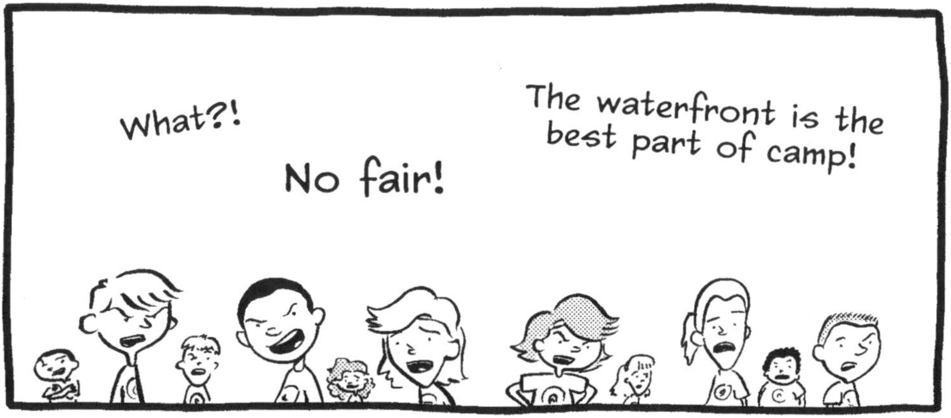
What?!
No fair!
The waterfront is the best part of camp!

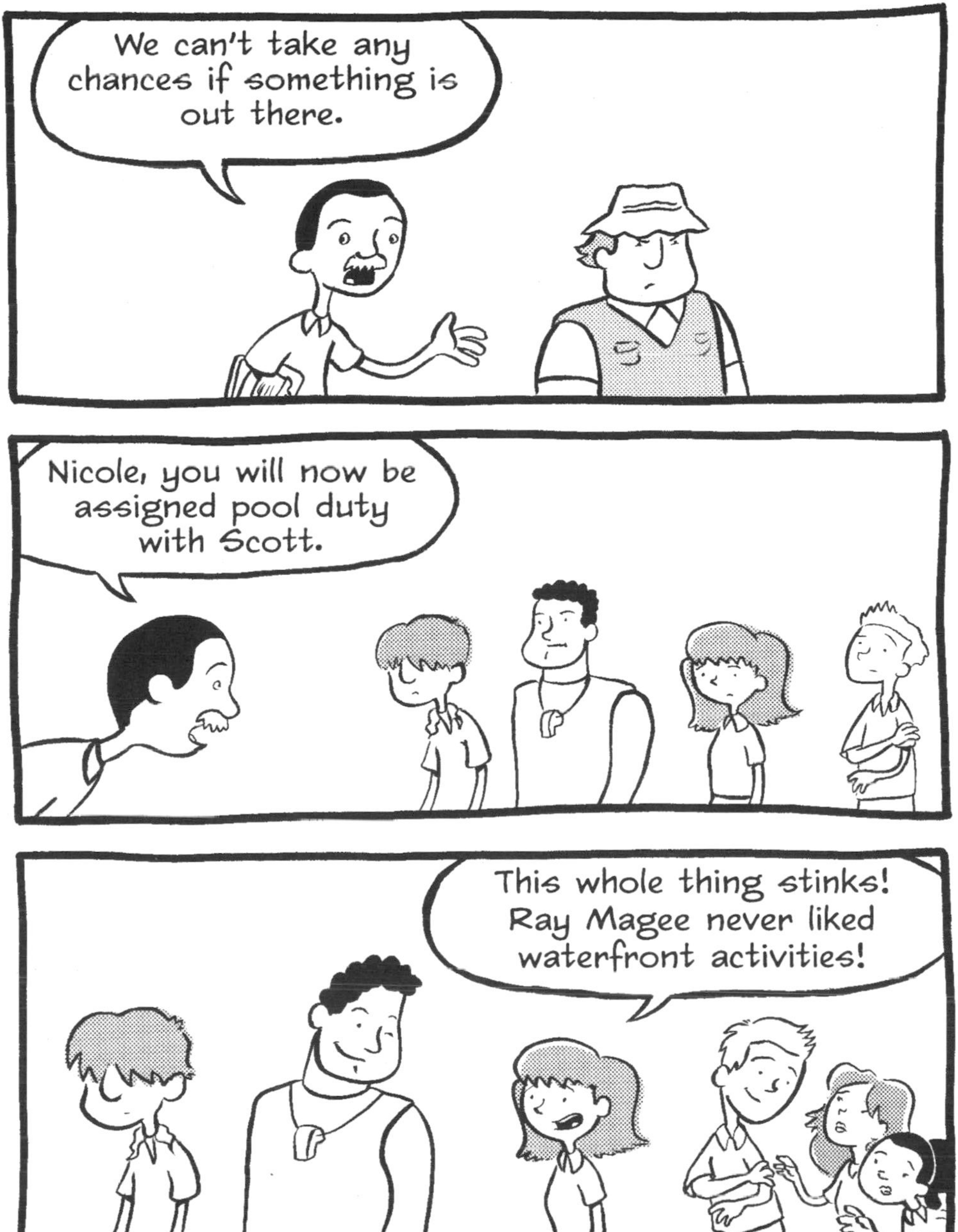
We can't take any chances if something is out there.
Nicole, you will now be assigned pool duty with Scott.
This whole thing stinks! Ray Magee never liked waterfront activities!

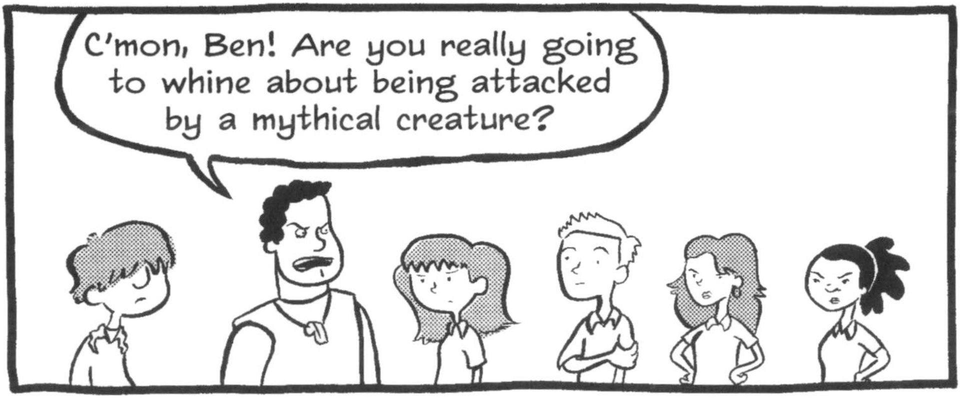
C'mon, Ben! Are you really going to whine about being attacked by a mythical creature?

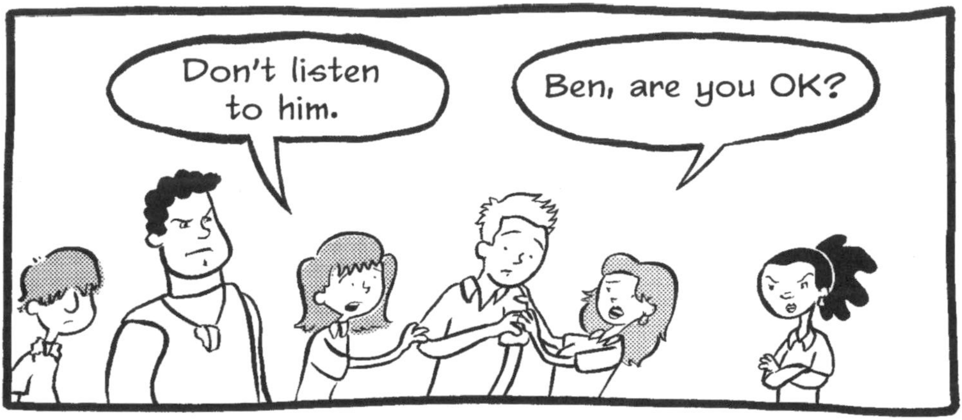
Don't listen to him.
Ben, are you OK?

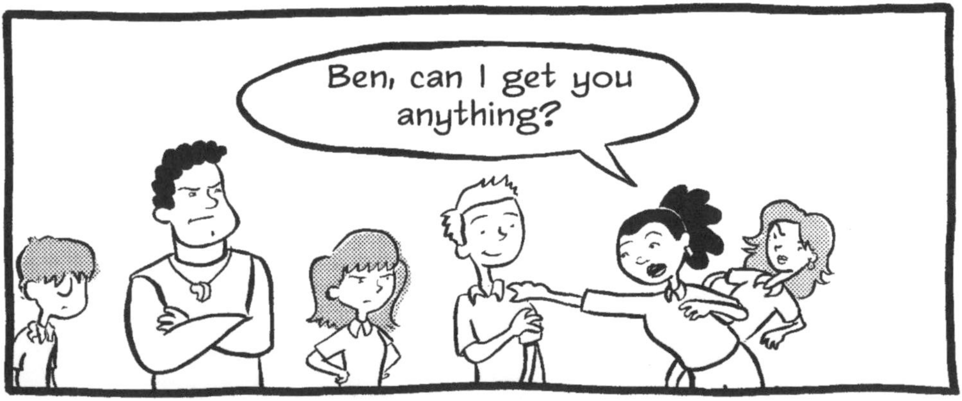
Ben, can I get you anything?

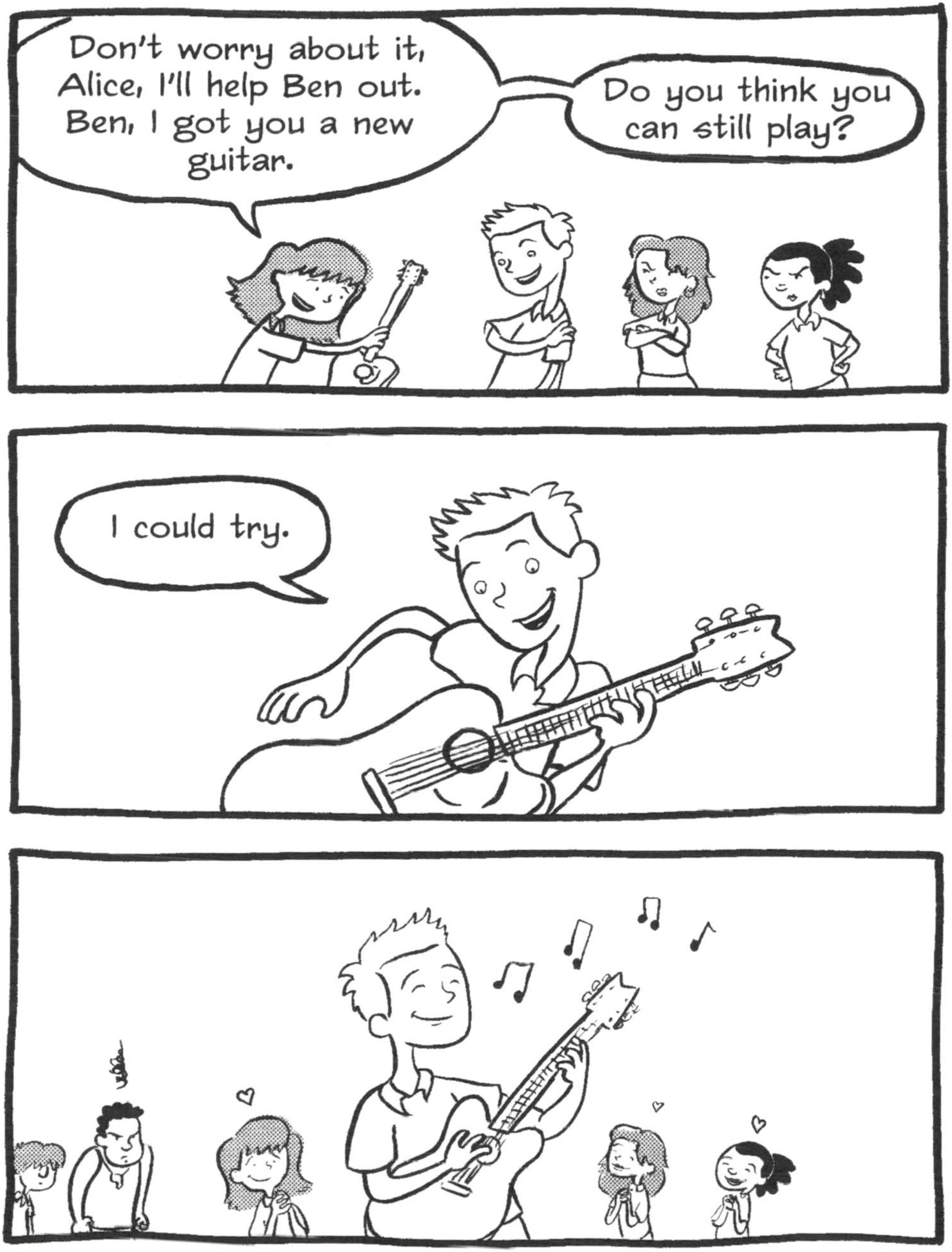

Don't worry about it, Alice, I'll help Ben out. Ben, I got you a new guitar.
Do you think you can still play?
I could try.

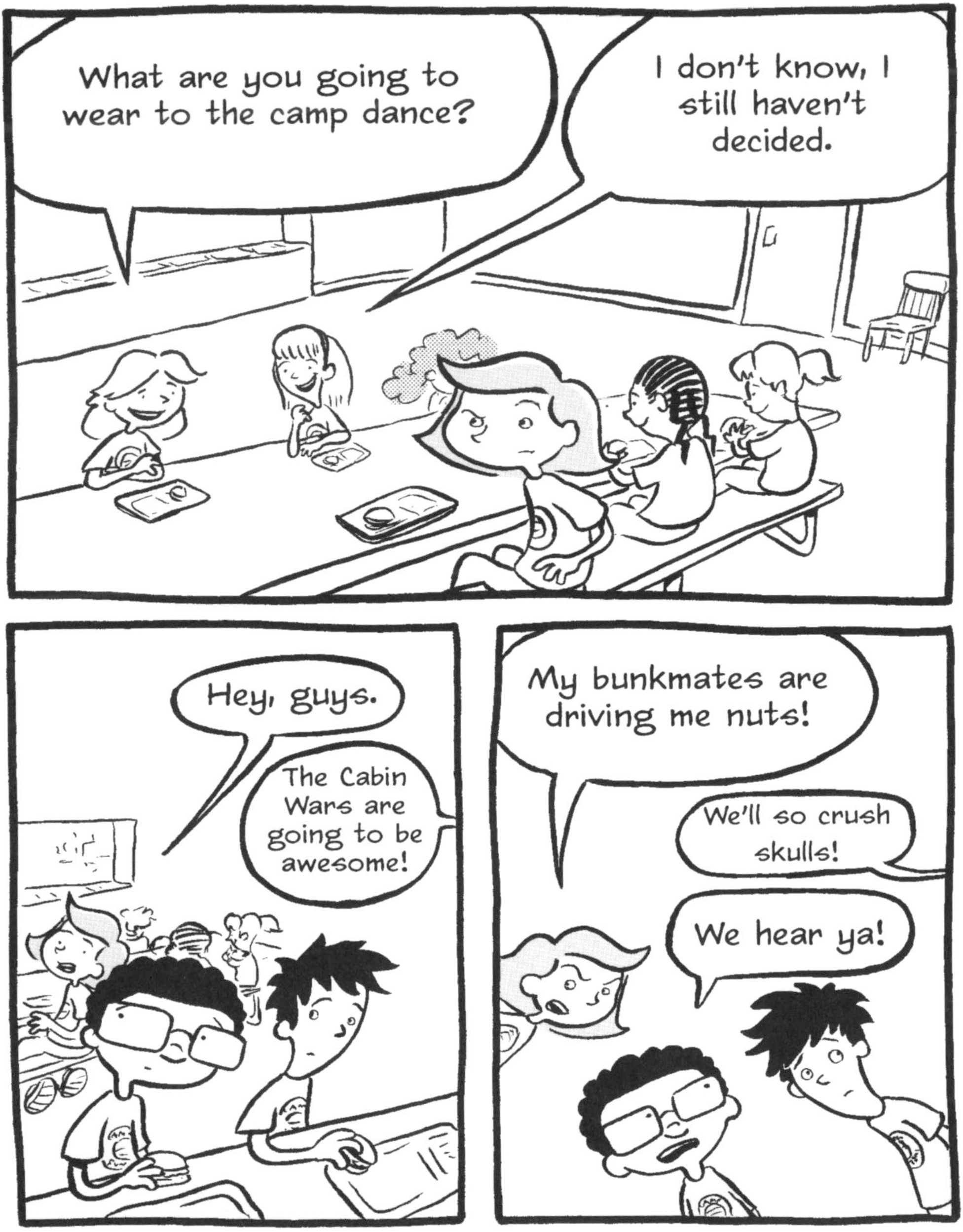
What are you going to wear to the camp dance?
I don't know, I still haven't decided.
Hey, guys.
The Cabin Wars are going to be awesome!
My bunkmates are driving me nuts!
We'll so crush skulls!
We hear ya!

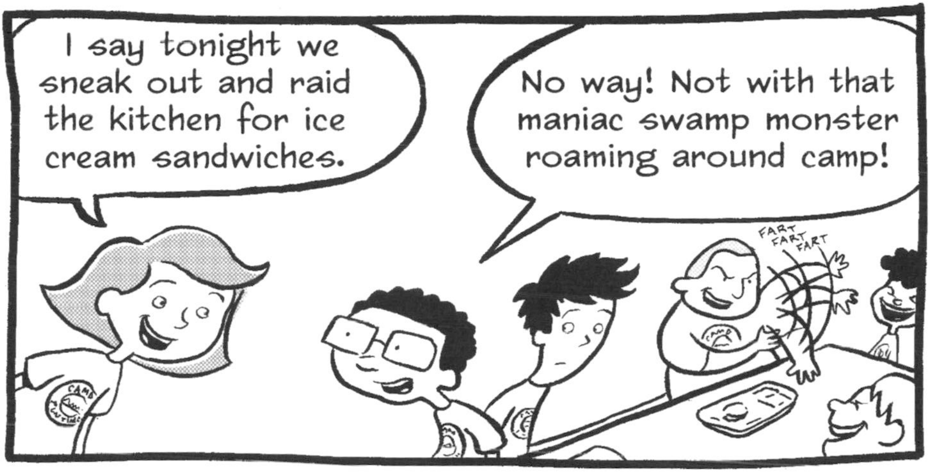
I say tonight we sneak out and raid the kitchen for ice cream sandwiches.
No way! Not with that maniac swamp monster roaming around camp!
FART FART FART

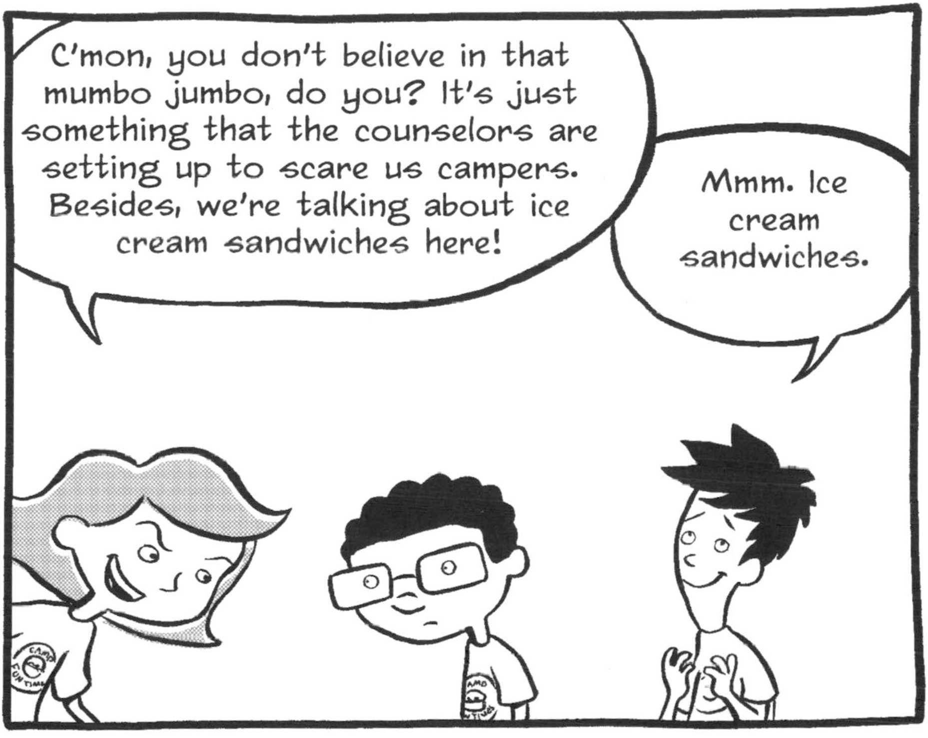
C'mon, you don't believe in that mumbo jumbo, do you? It's just something that the counselors are setting up to scare us campers. Besides, we're talking about ice cream sandwiches here!
Mmm. Ice cream sandwiches.

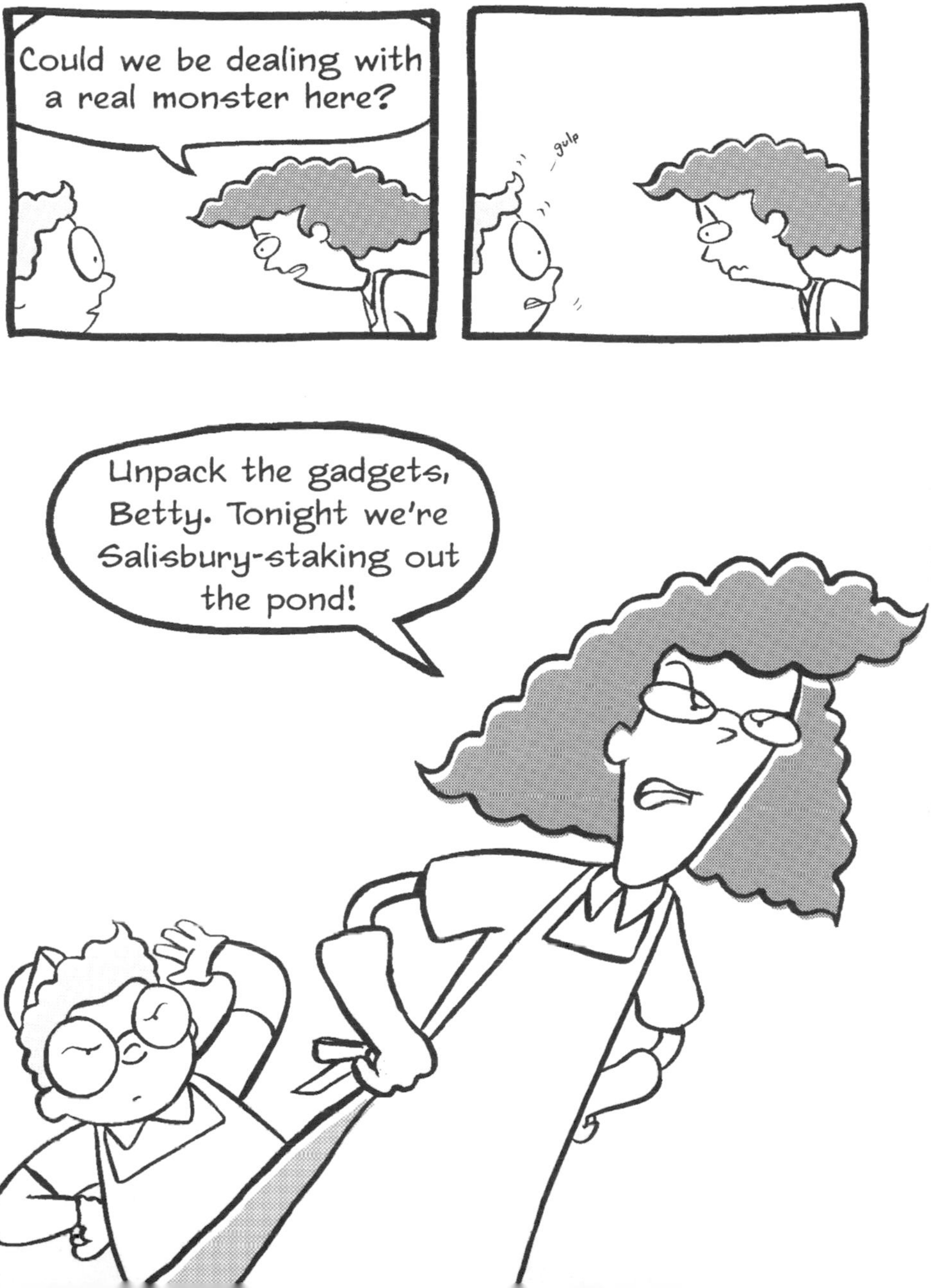
Could we be dealing with a real monster here?
gulp
Unpack the gadgets, Betty. Tonight we're Salisbury-staking out the pond!

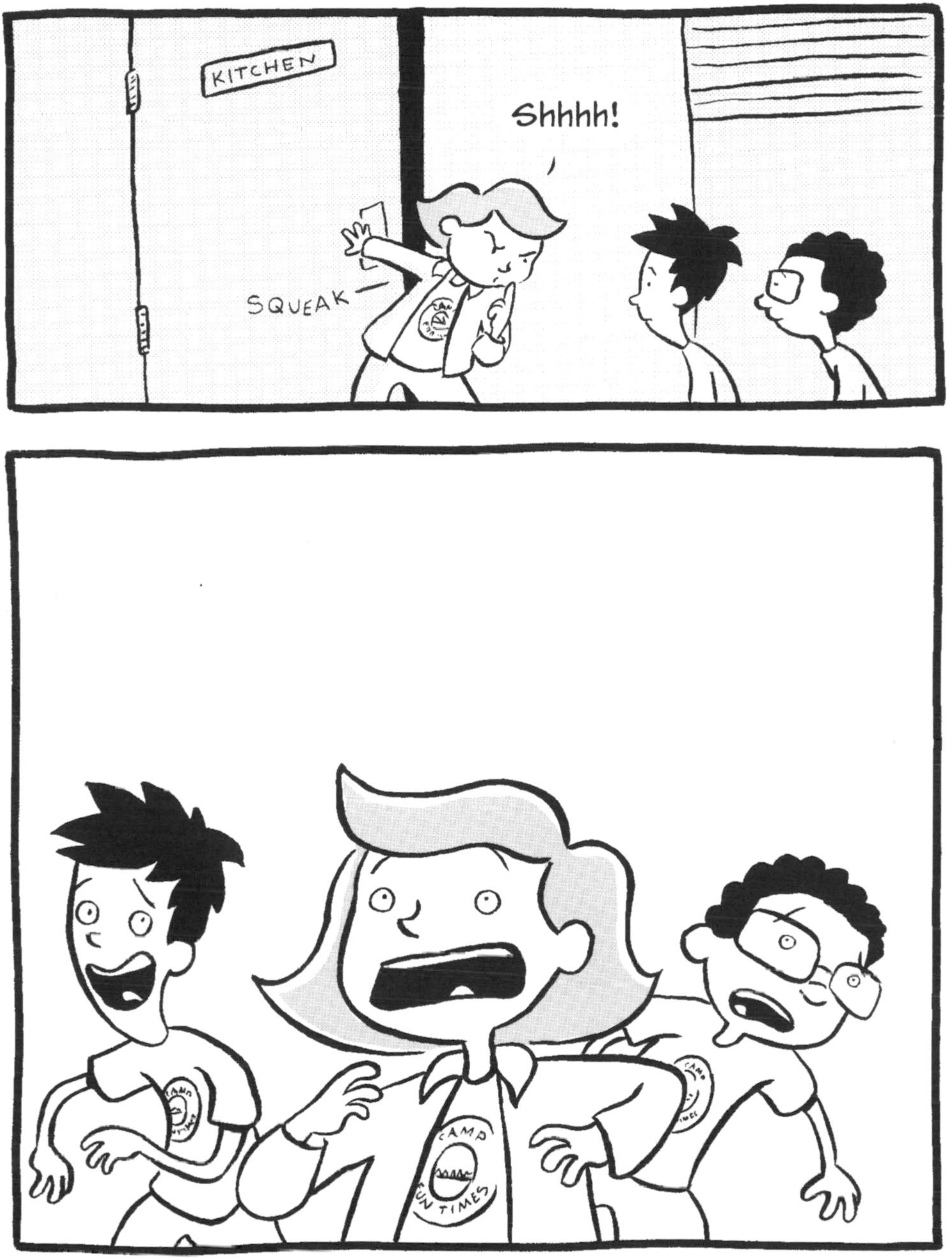
KITCHEN
Shhhh!
SQUEAK

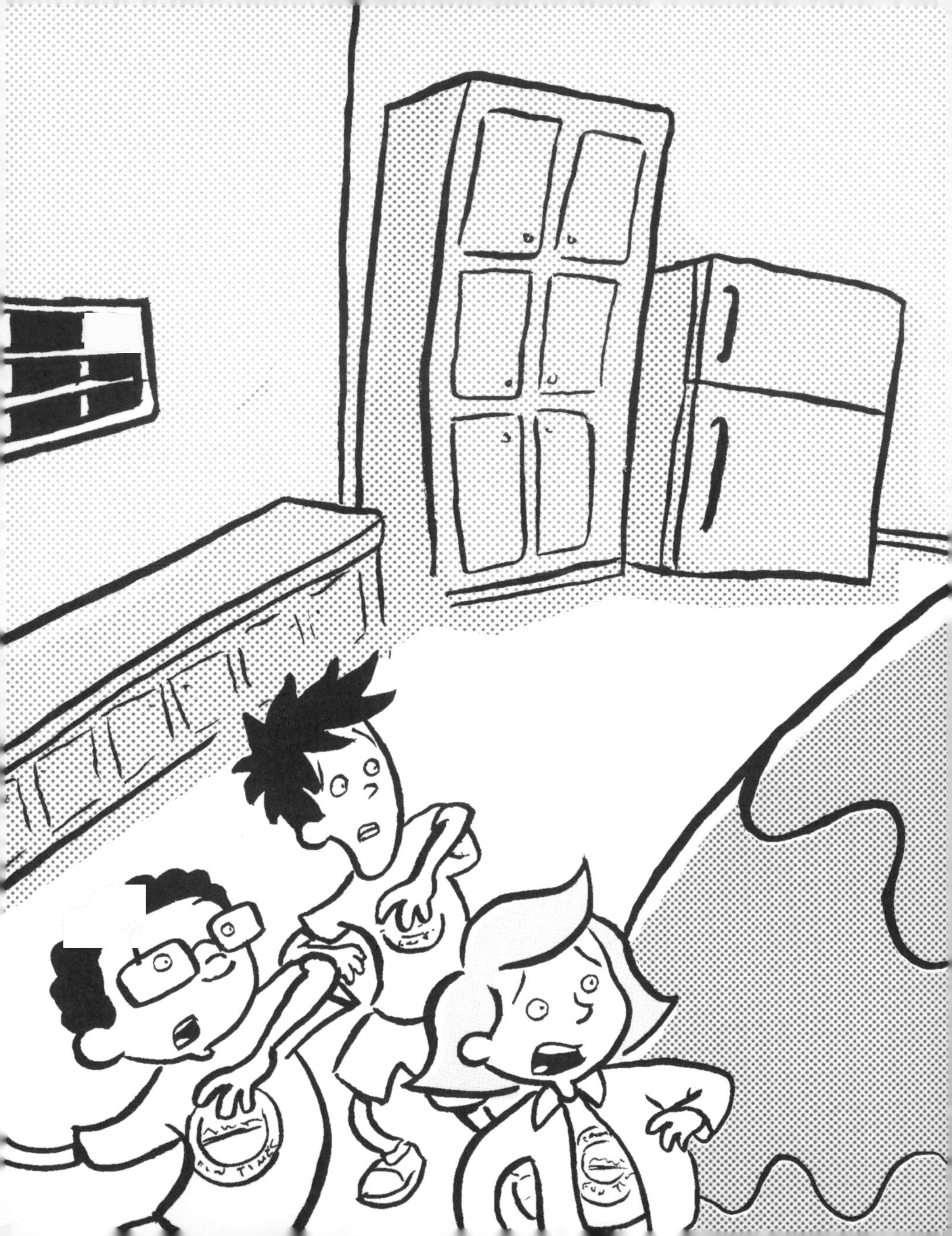

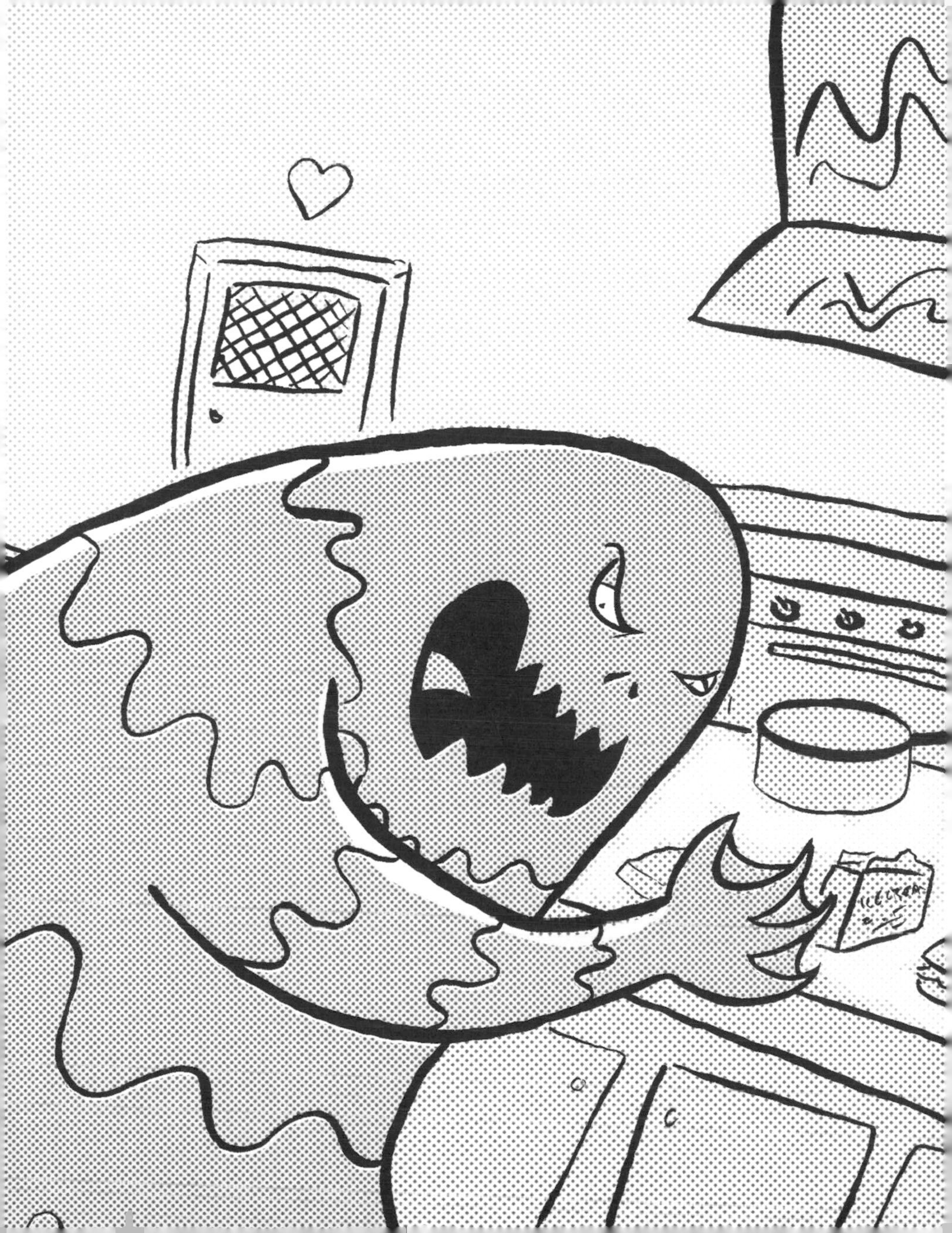
ICE CREAM

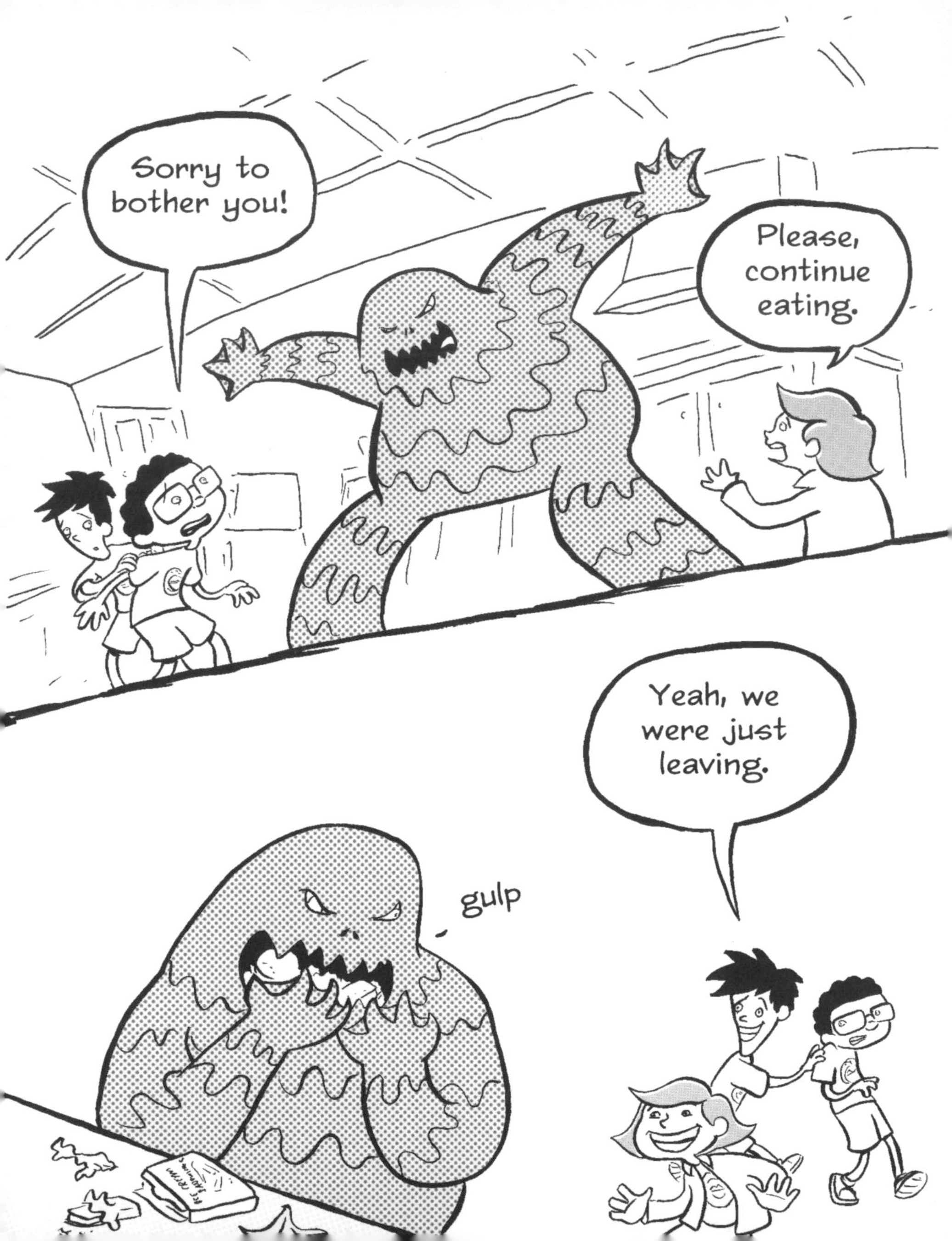
Sorry to bother you!
Please, continue eating.
Yeah, we were just leaving.
gulp

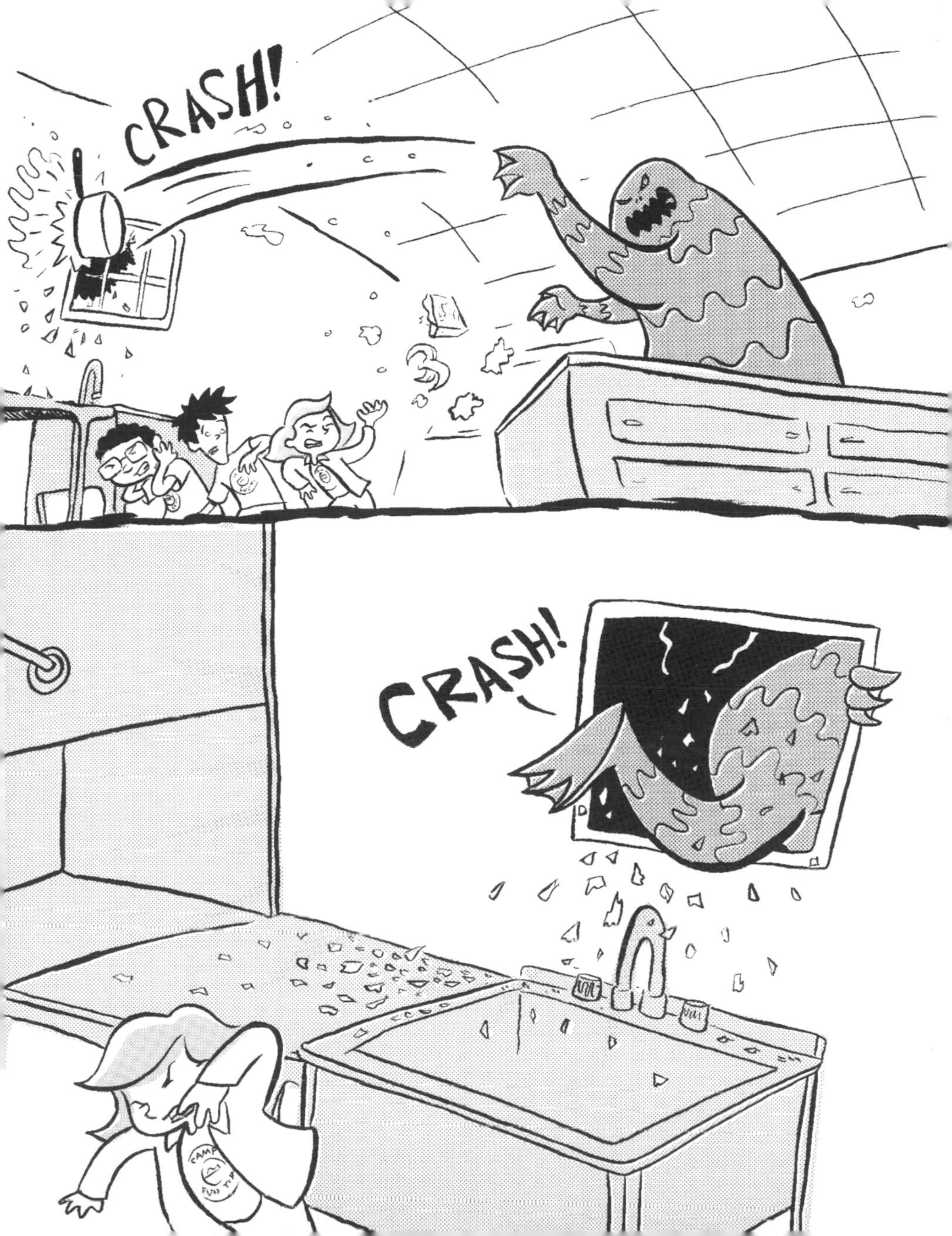
CRASH!
CRASH!

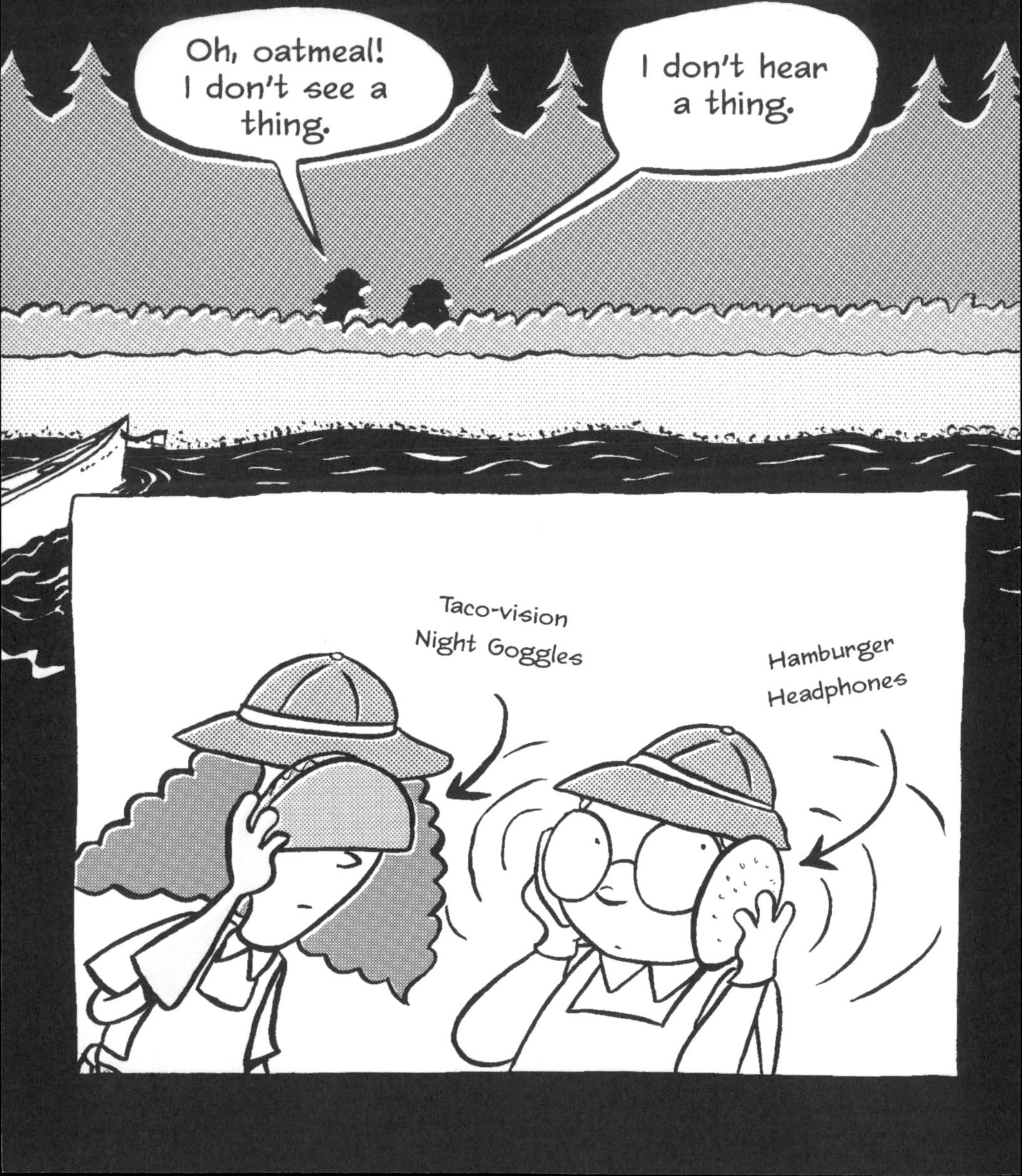
Oh, oatmeal! I don't see a thing.
I don't hear a thing.
Taco-vision Night Goggles
Hamburger Headphones

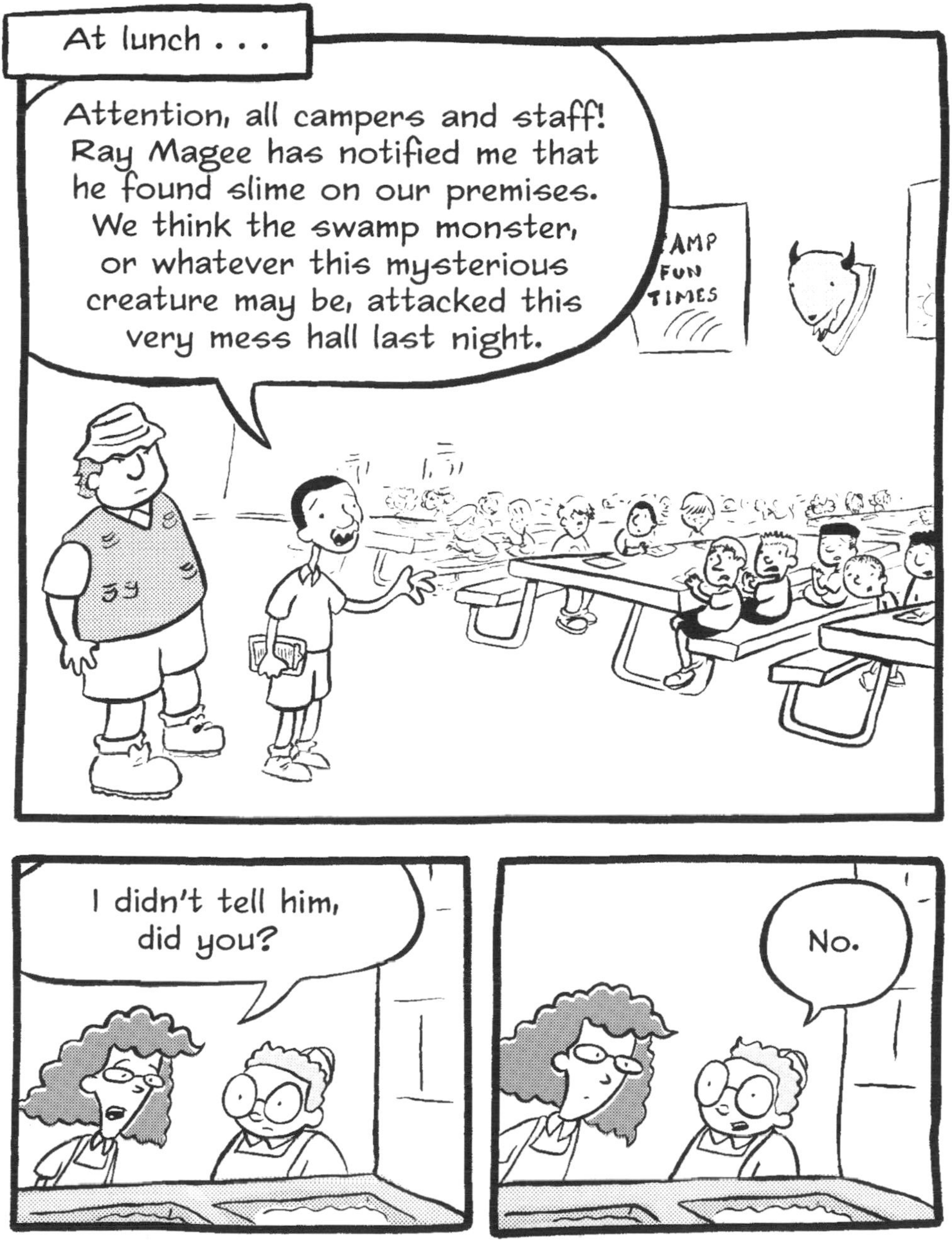
At lunch . . .
Attention, all campers and staff! Ray Magee has notified me that he found slime on our premises. We think the swamp monster, or whatever this mysterious creature may be, attacked this very mess hall last night.
CAMP FUN TIMES
I didn't tell him, did you?
No.

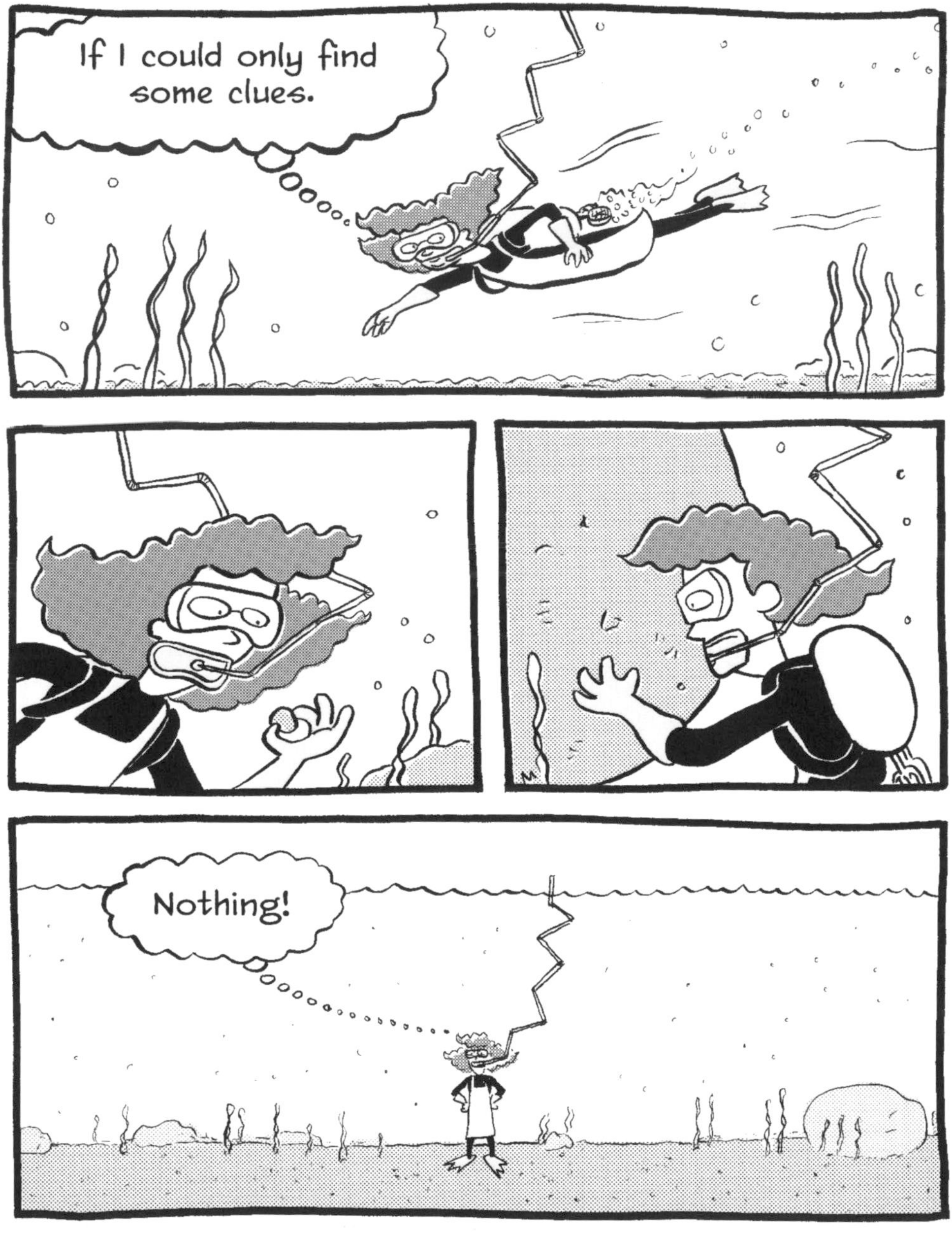
If I could only find some clues.
Nothing!

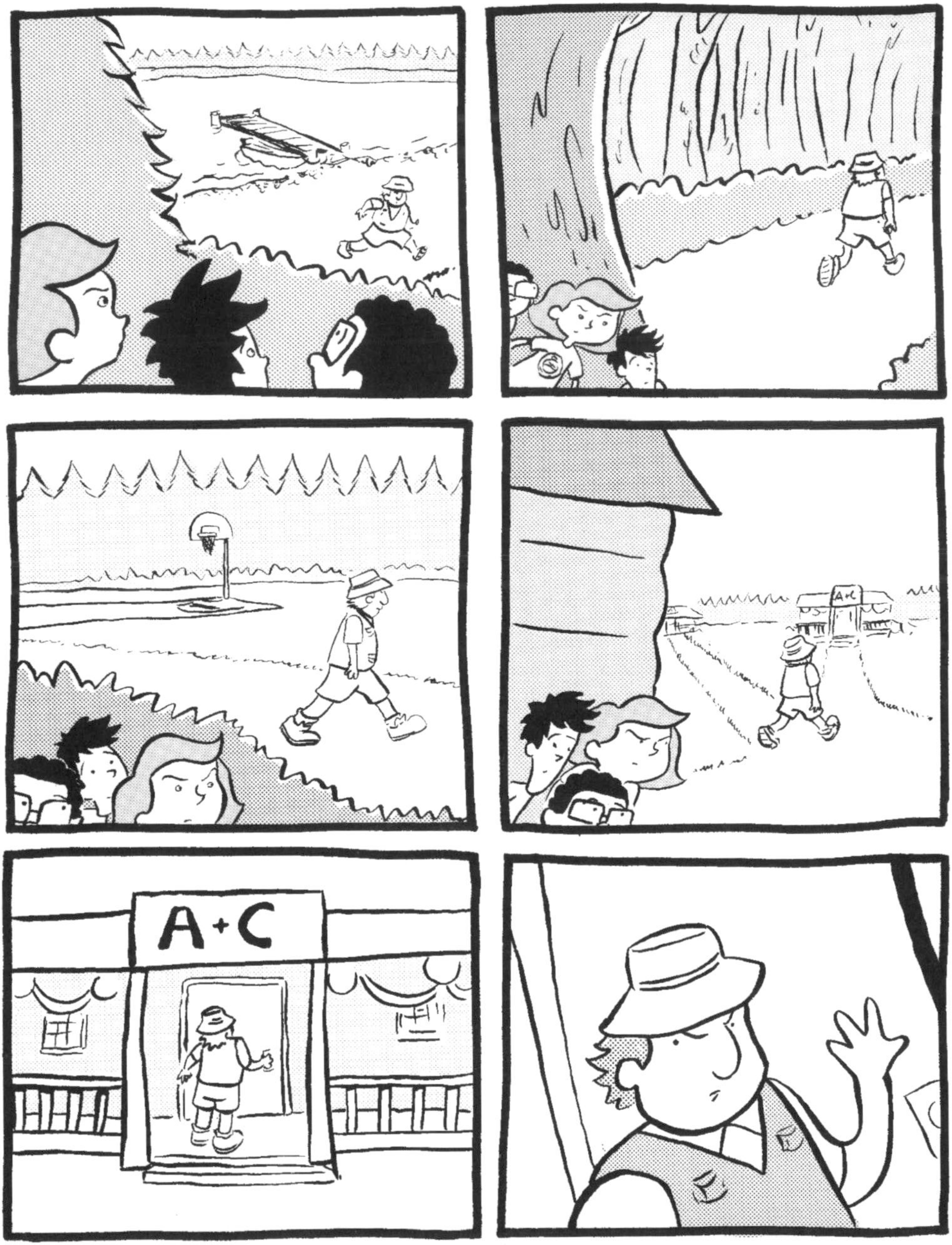
A+C

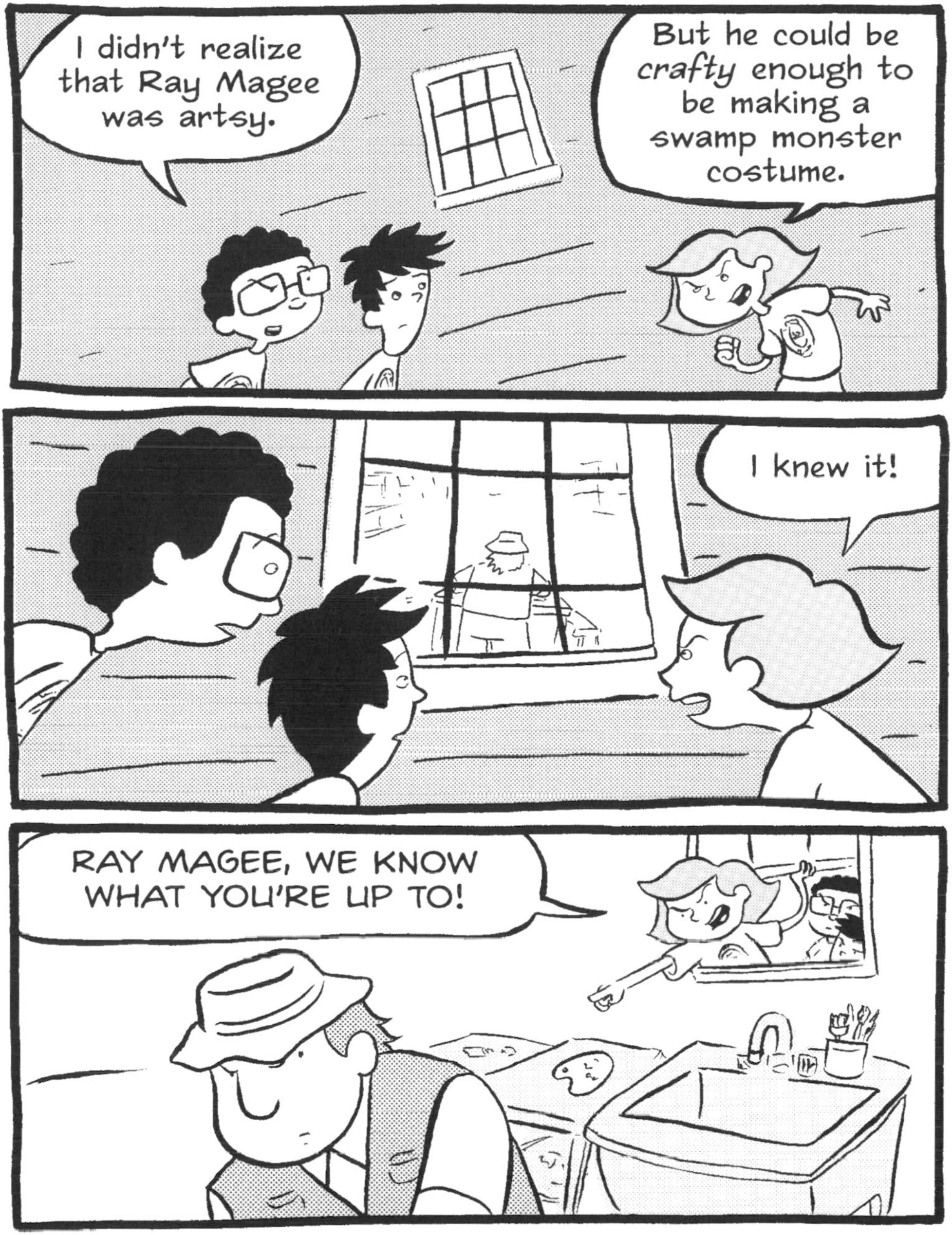
I didn't realize that Ray Magee was artsy.
But he could be *crafty* enough to be making a swamp monster costume.
I knew it!
RAY MAGEE, WE KNOW WHAT YOU'RE UP TO!

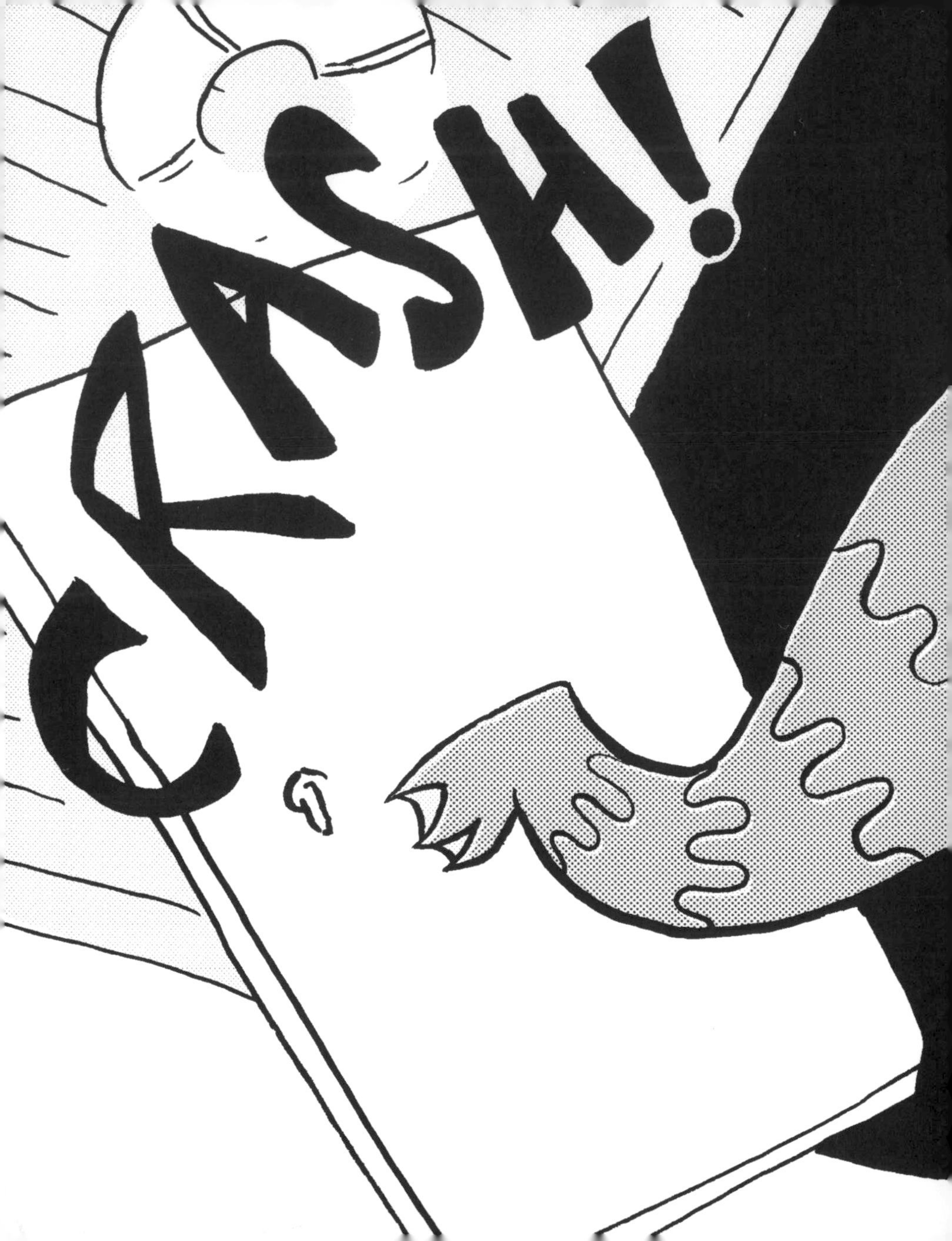
CRASH!

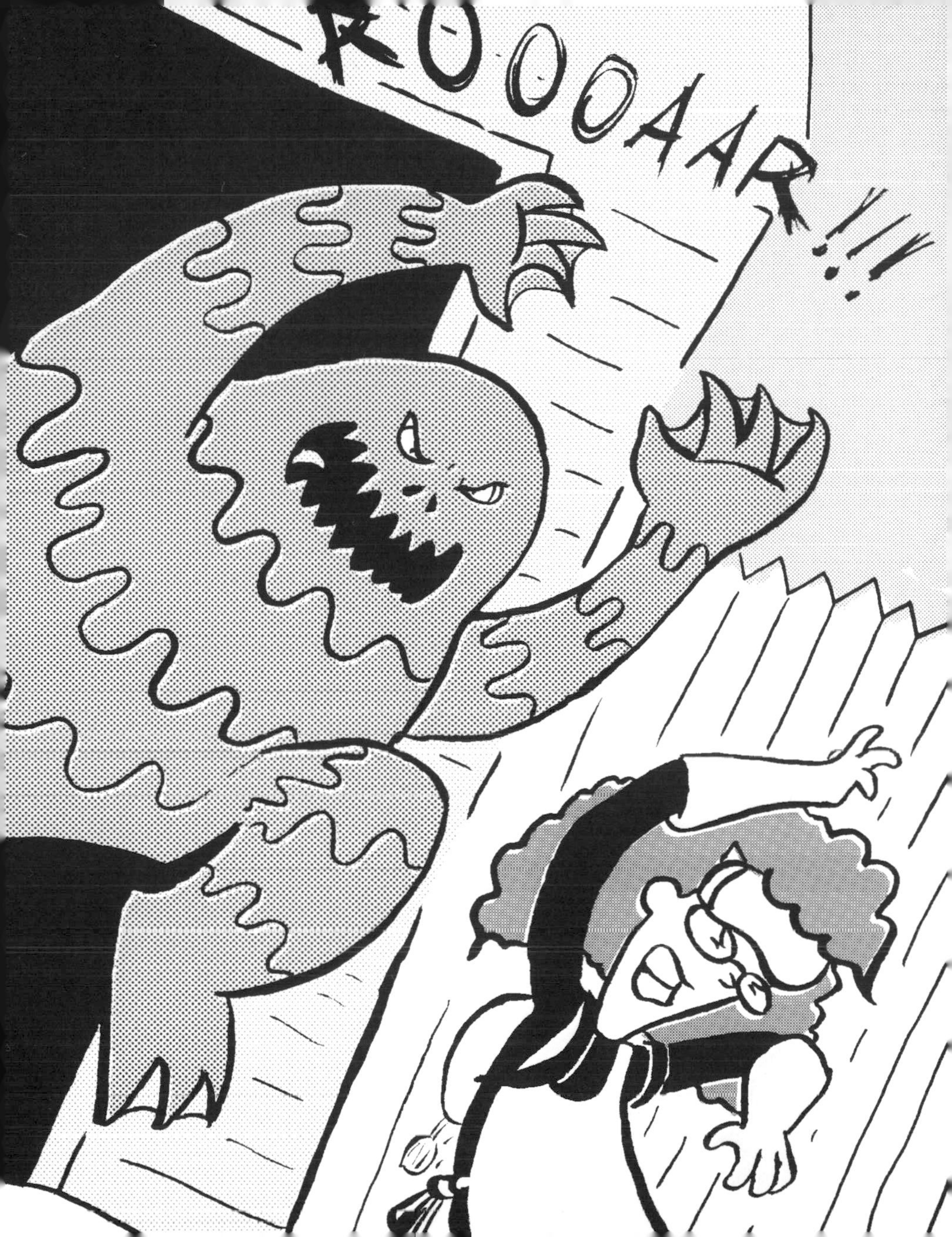
ROOOAAR!!!

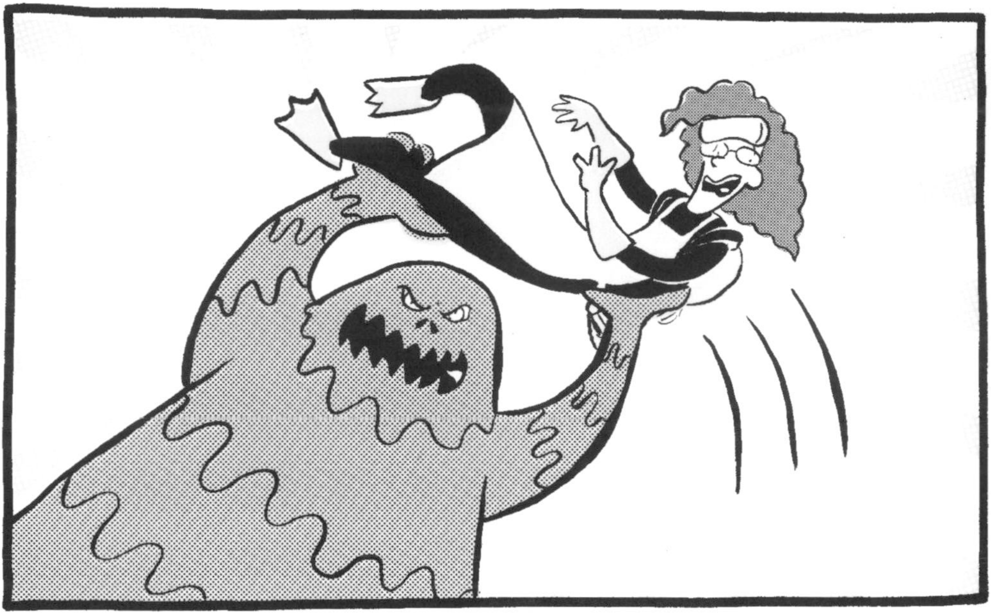

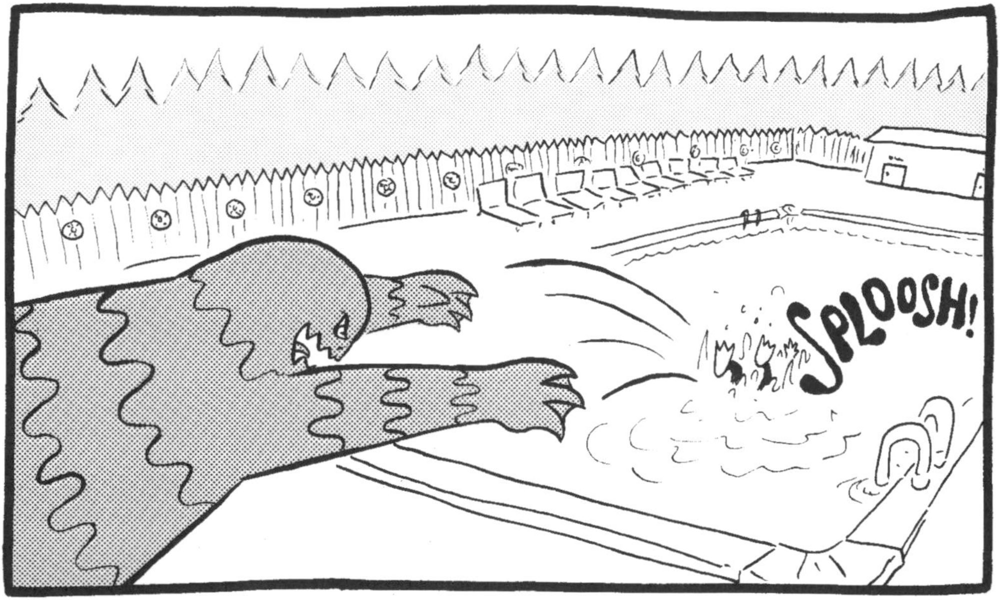
SPLOOSH!

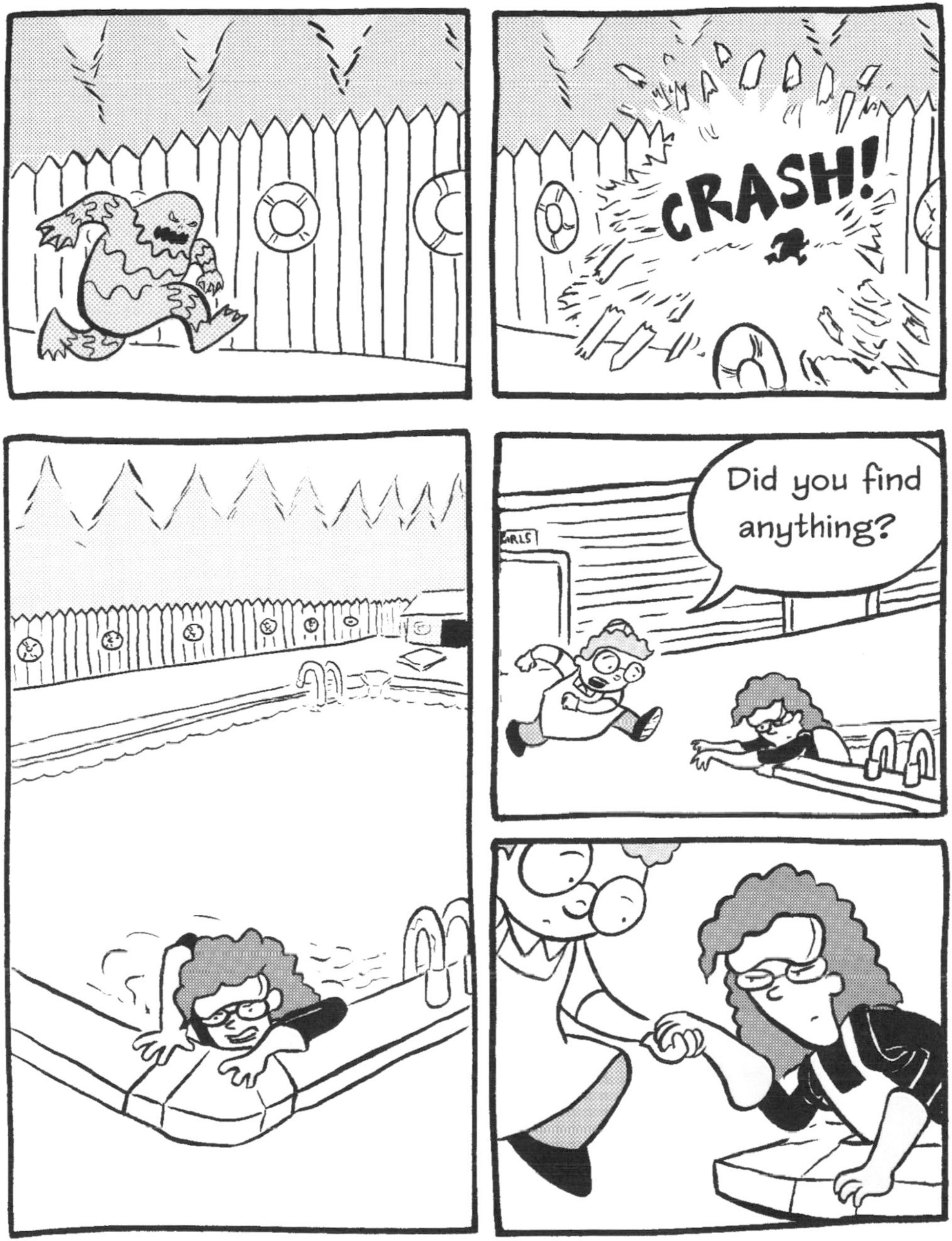
CRASH!
GIRLS
Did you find anything?

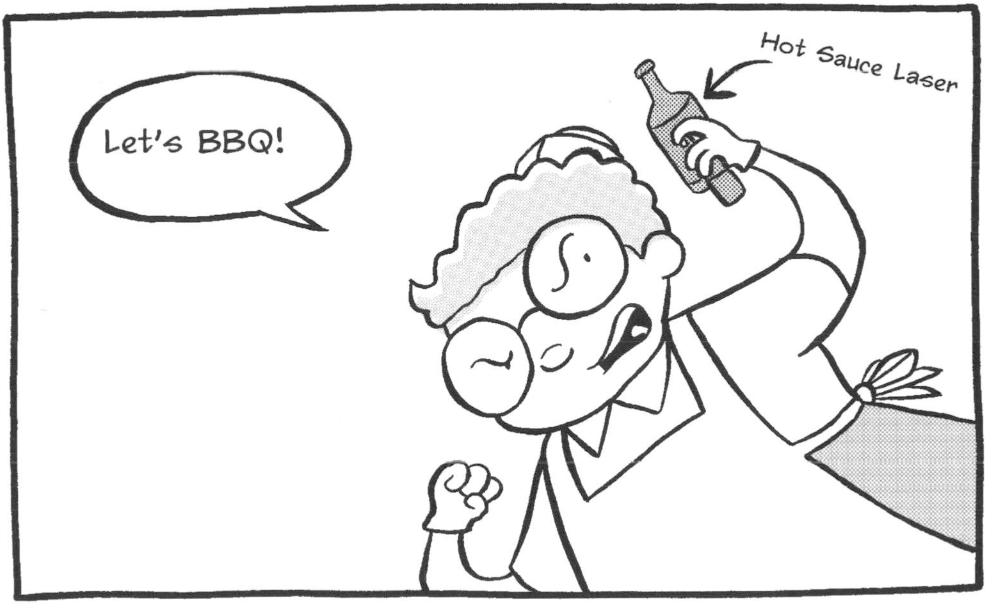
Let's BBQ!
Hot Sauce Laser

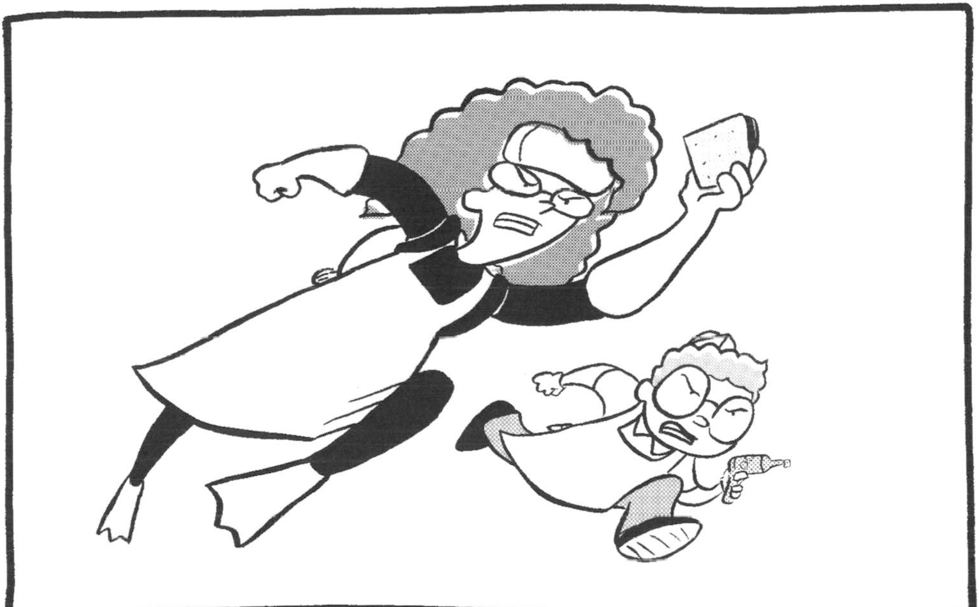

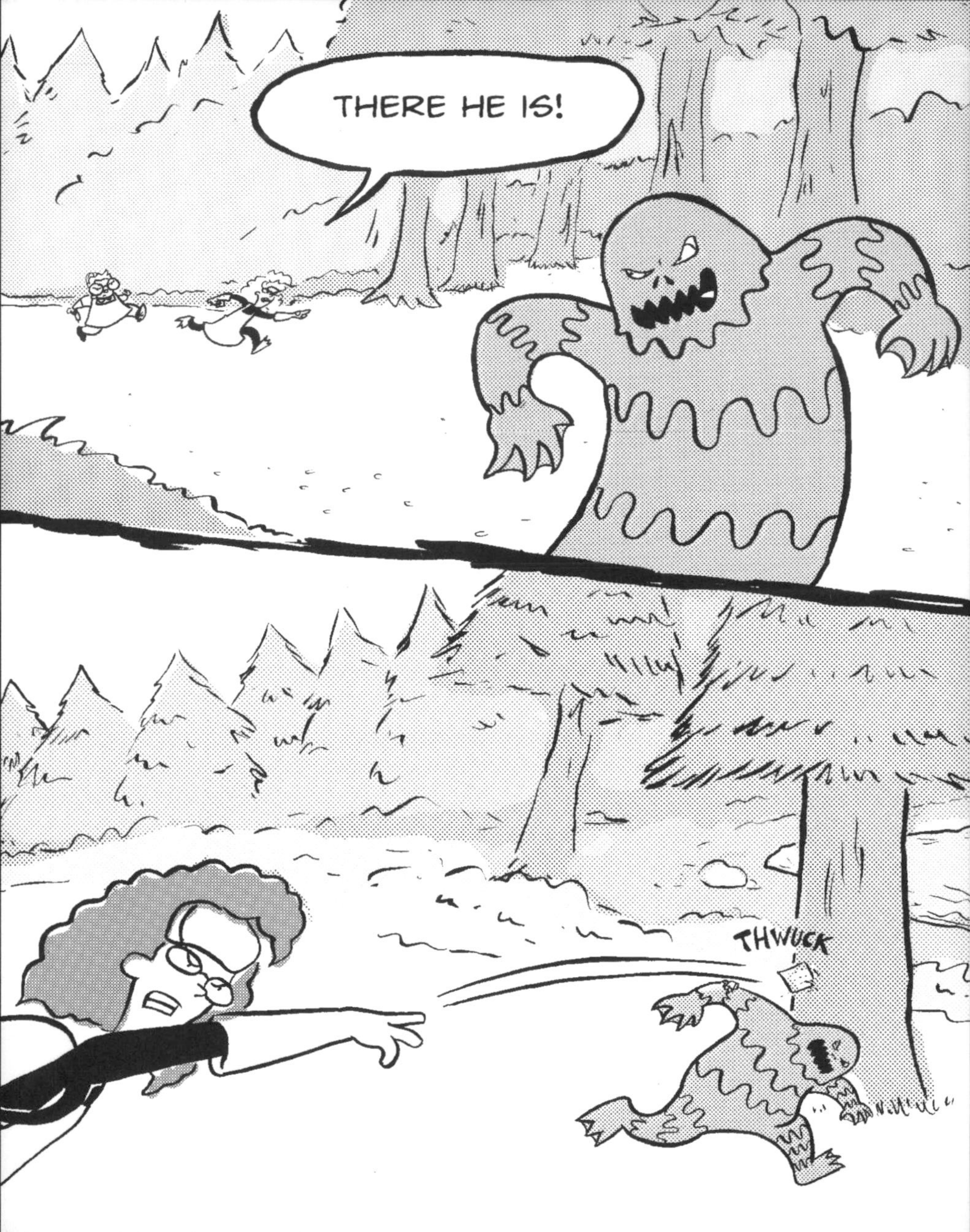
THERE HE IS!
THWUCK

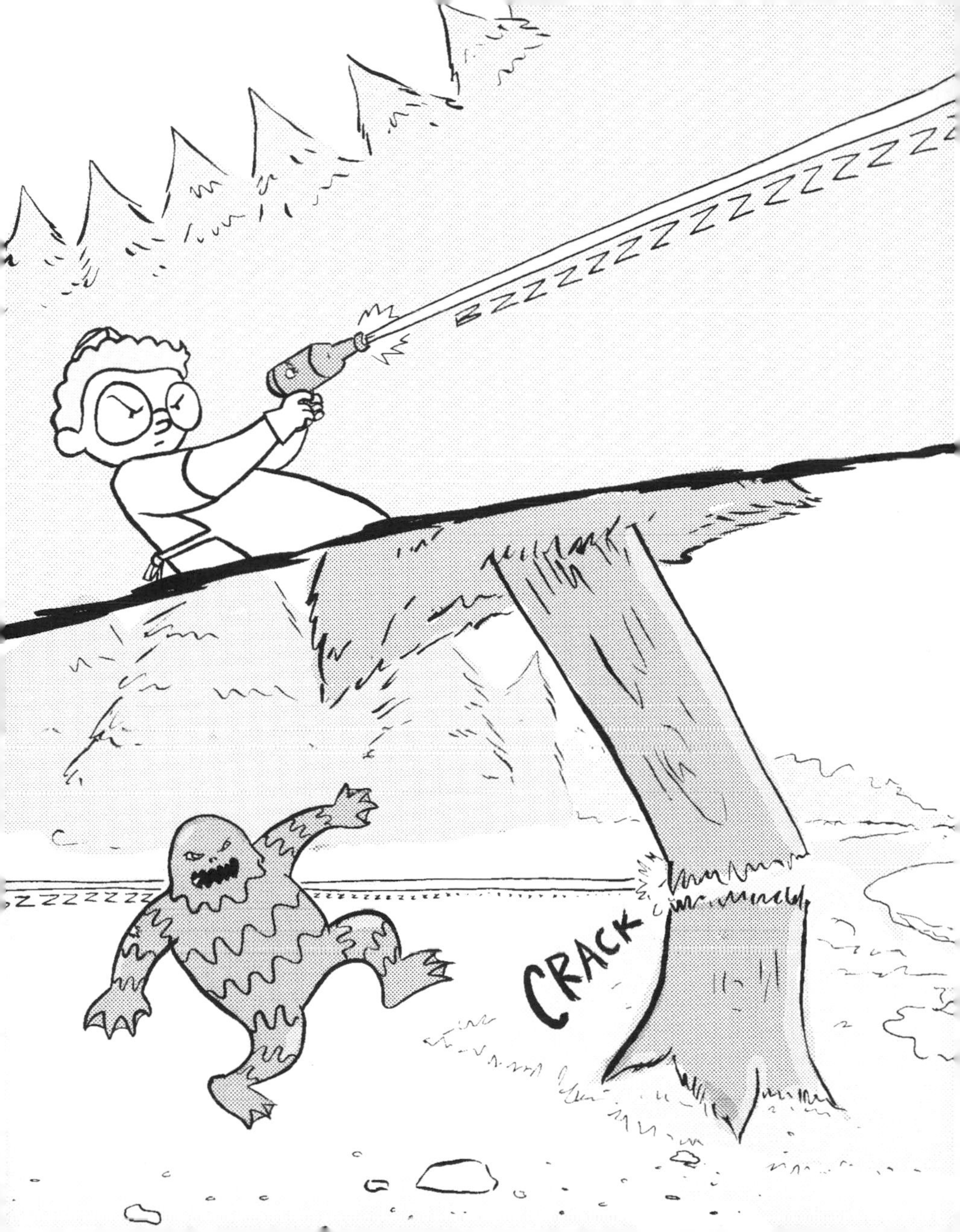

BZZZZZZZZZZZZZZZZZZZ
ZZZZZZZZ
CRACK

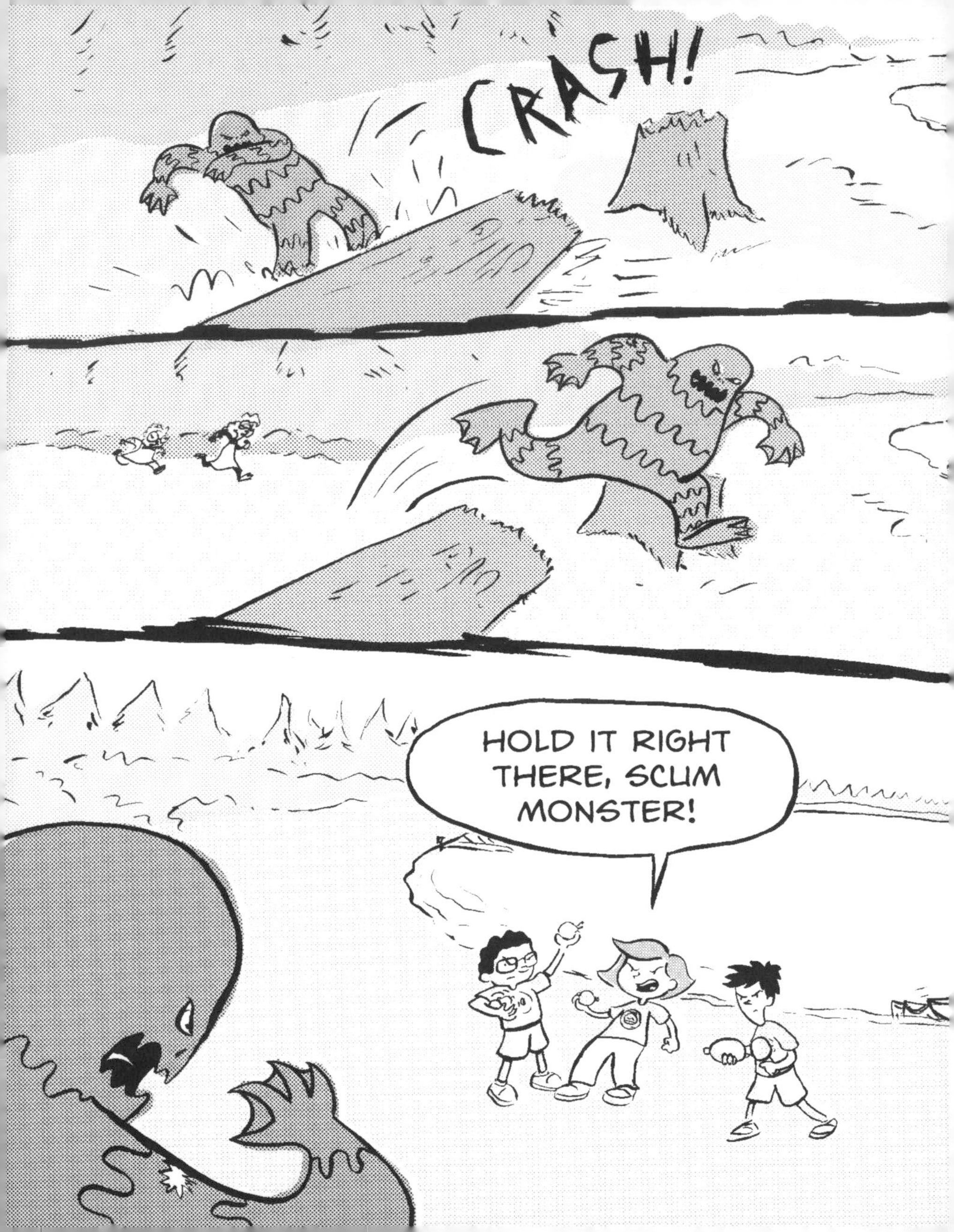
CRASH!
HOLD IT RIGHT THERE, SCUM MONSTER!

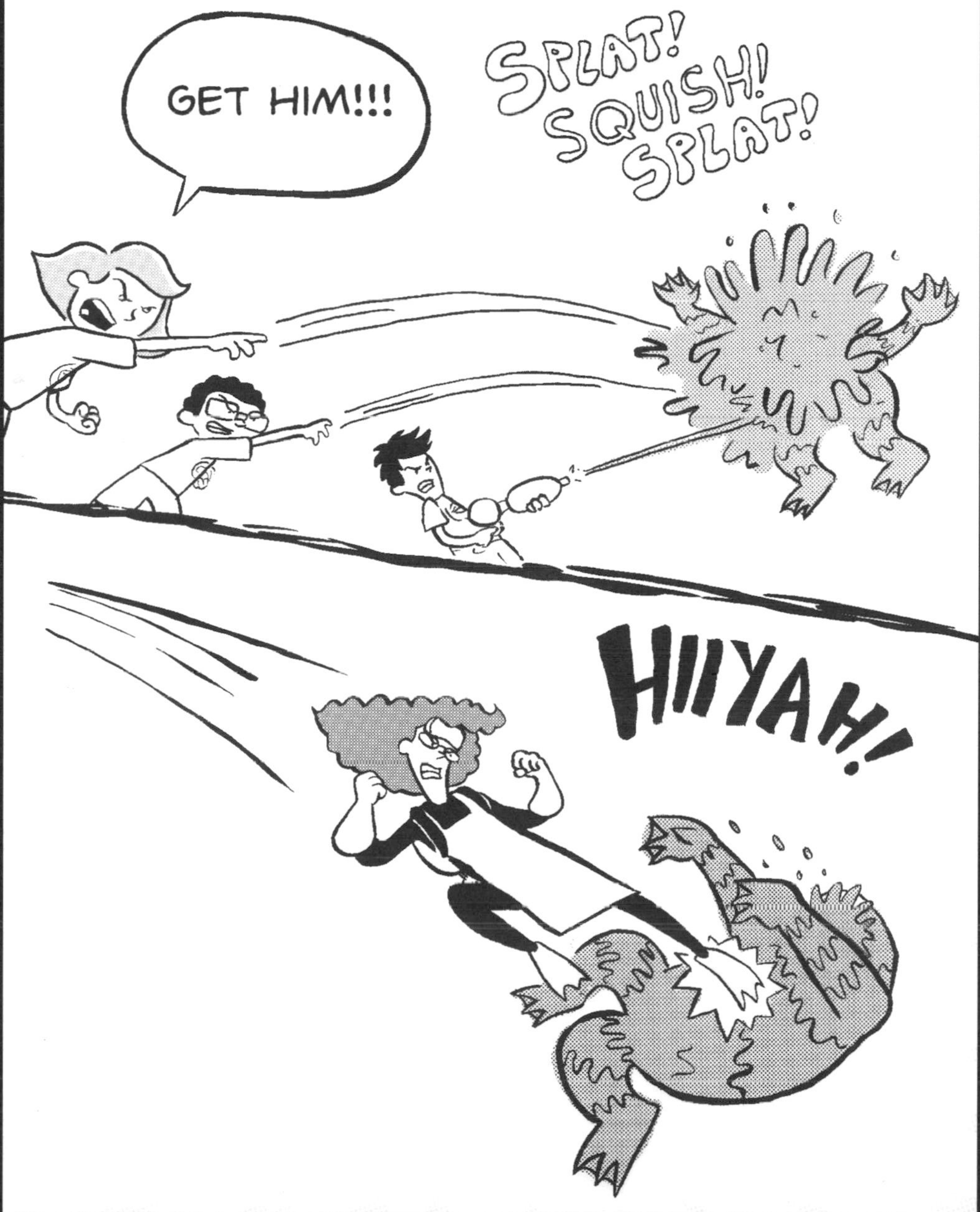
GET HIM!!!
SPLAT! SQUISH! SPLAT!
HIIYAH!!

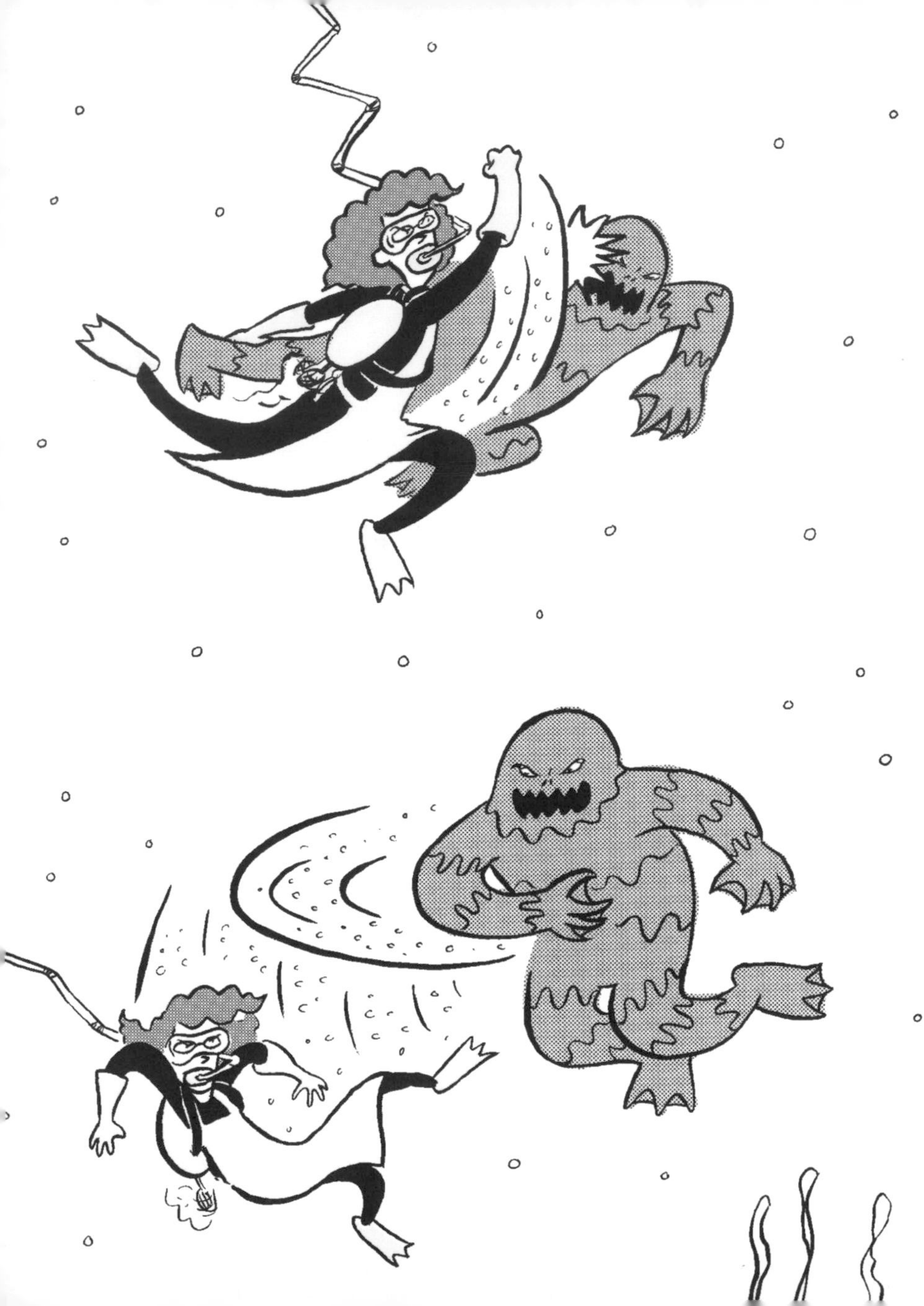

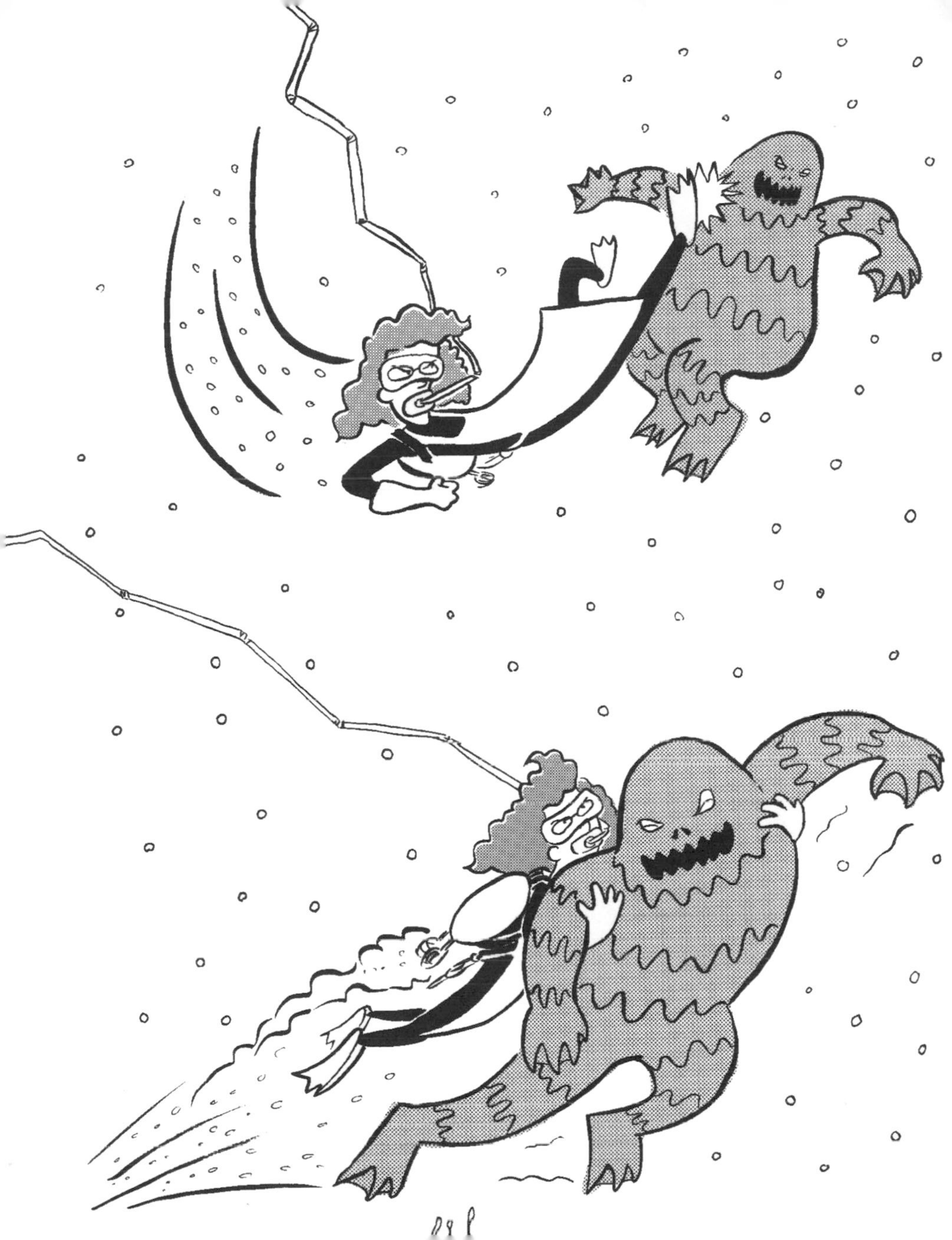

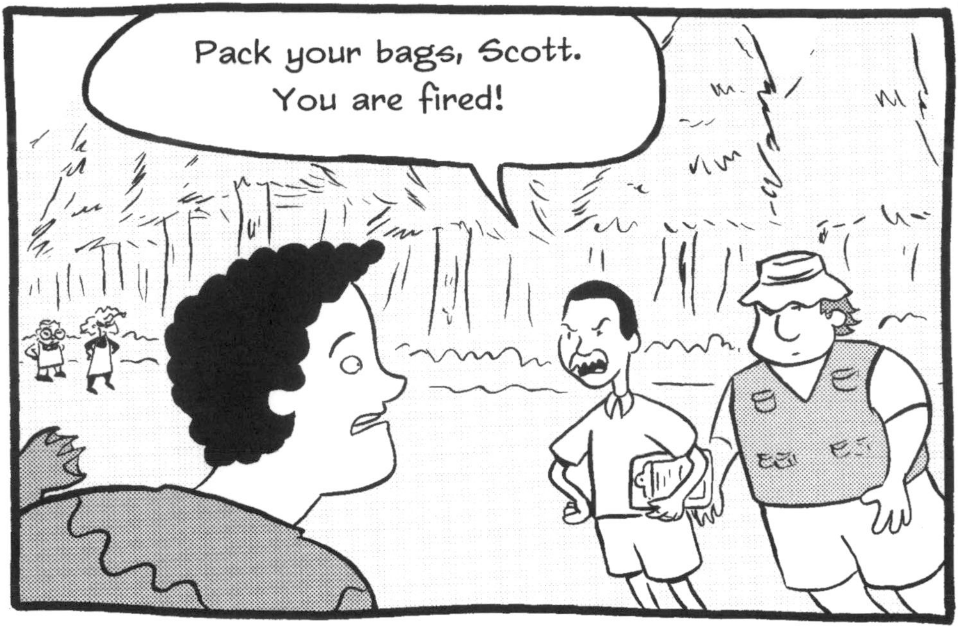
Pack your bags, Scott. You are fired!

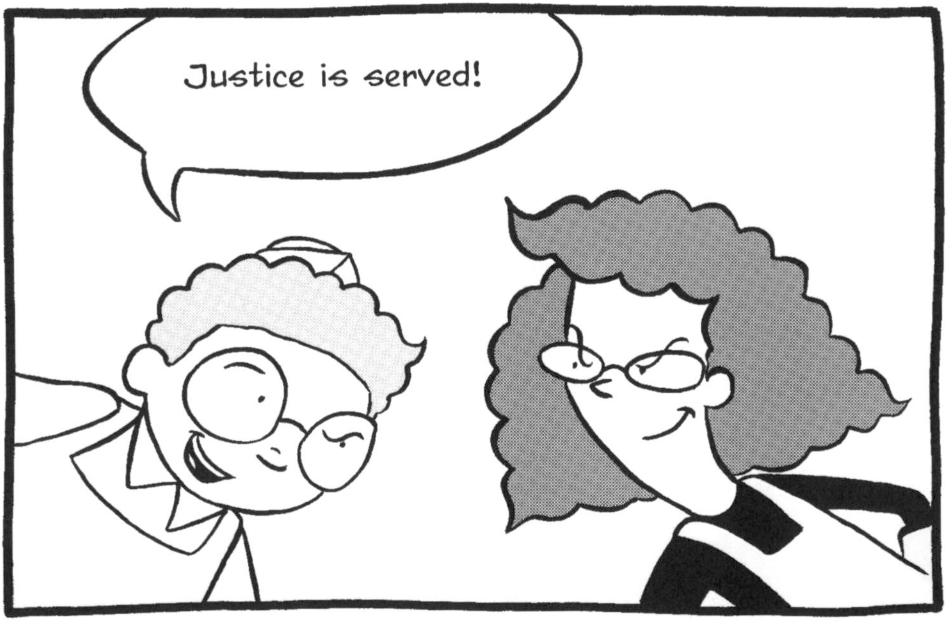
Justice is served!

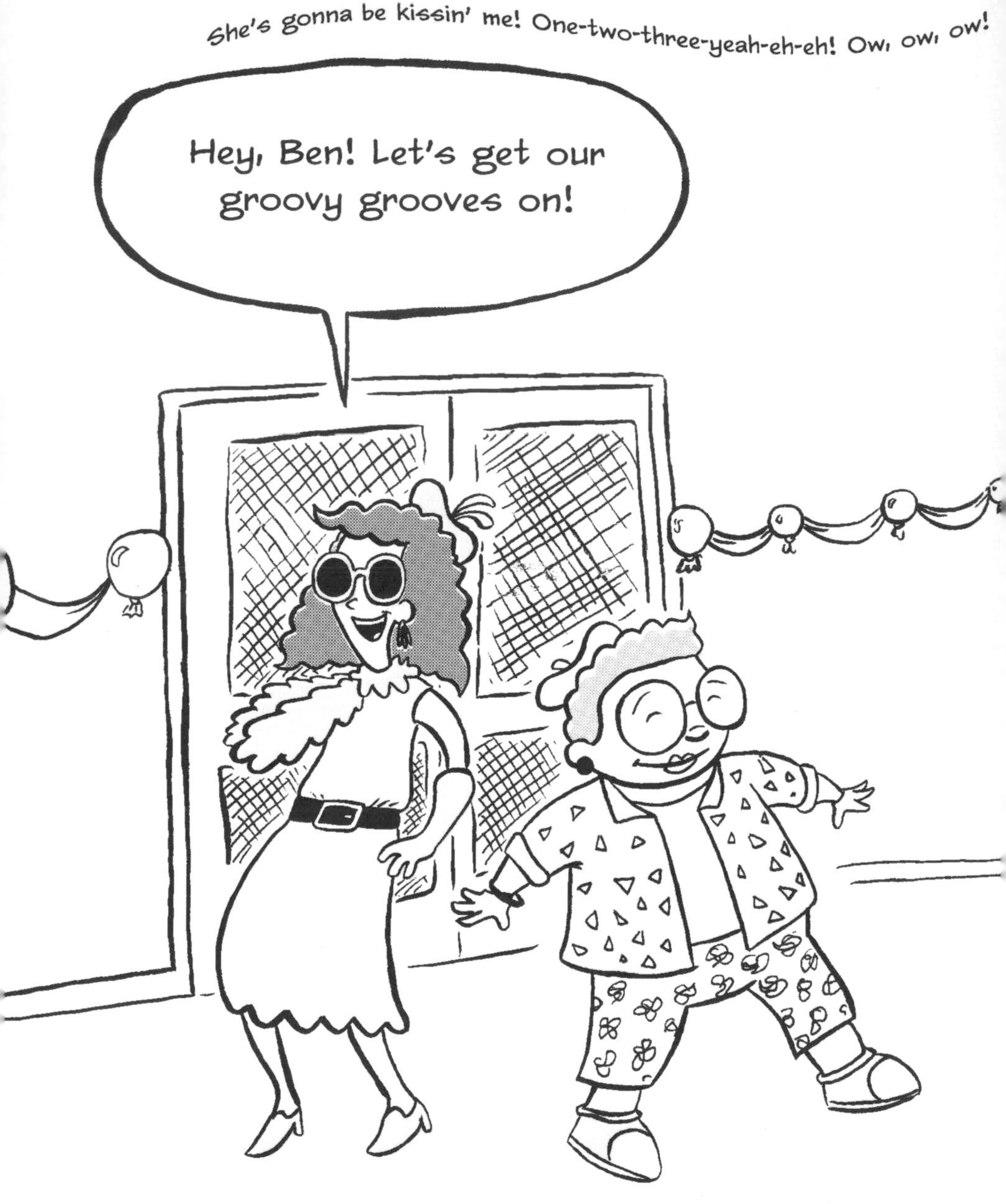
She's gonna be kissin' me! One-two-three-yeah-eh-eh! Ow, ow, ow!
Hey, Ben! Let's get our groovy grooves on!

FOR ALL OF MY FRIENDS FROM
THE HOLE IN THE WALL GANG CAMP.
—J.J.K.

THIS IS A BORZOI BOOK PUBLISHED BY ALFRED A. KNOPF

All rights reserved. Published in the United States by Alfred A. Knopf, an imprint of Random House Children's Books, a division of Random House, Inc., New York.

Knopf, Borzoi Books, and the colophon are registered trademarks of Random House, Inc.

Visit us on the Web! www.randomhouse.com/kids

Educators and librarians, for a variety of teaching tools,
visit us at www.randomhouse.com/teachers

Library of Congress Cataloging-in-Publication Data
Krosoczka, Jarrett J.
Lunch Lady and the summer camp shakedown / Jarrett J. Krosoczka. — 1st ed.
p. cm.
Summary: When the crime-fighting school lunch lady works as the cook at summer camp,
she investigates the mystery of the legendary swamp monster.
ISBN 978-0-375-86095-9 (trade pbk.) — ISBN 978-0-375-96095-6 (lib. bdg.)
1. Graphic novels. [1. Graphic novels. 2. Camps—Fiction. 3. Mystery and detective stories.]
I. Title.
PZ7.7.K76Lus 2010
741.5'973—dc22
2009039783

The text of this book is set in Hedge Backwards.
The illustrations in this book were created using ink on paper and digital coloring.

MANUFACTURED IN MALAYSIA
May 2010
10 9 8 7 6 5 4

First Edition